CW00859784

THE LAST GENERATION

The Book Guild Ltd

First published in Great Britain in 2021 by
The Book Guild Ltd
9 Priory Business Park
Wistow Road, Kibworth
Leicestershire, LE8 0RX
Freephone: 0800 999 2982
www.bookguild.co.uk
Email: info@bookguild.co.uk
Twitter: @bookguild

Typeset in 11pt Minion Pro

Printed and bound by CPI Group (UK) Ltd, Croydon, CR0 4YY

ISBN 978 1913551 681

British Library Cataloguing in Publication Data.
A catalogue record for this book is available from the British Library.

For Dave & Gerry

ONE

Mrs Atkinson ran a tight ship at Oakham Elementary. She could be hard but always demonstrated fair play. At least, that was in her opinion. It was, moreover, the opinion shared by most of the students and other staff members as well. She certainly would not have believed it possible for a student, let alone two students, to be out of bed after curfew. It was late. She sat at her grand mahogany desk shrouded by candlelight, scrolling through the reams of documents on her tablet, with perfunctory sweeps of her right index finger.

'May I come in?' said a voice from the doorway.

In the same moment that Mrs Atkinson looked up from her work, Ellie Webster – a student of Oakham Elementary, who *was* out of bed after curfew – opened her eyes.

Ellie was, in fact, stood with her back pressed firmly against a tree, in the forest that bordered the school.

She had crept out from her dormitory to meet her best friend, Jake. It was not the first time she had done this. Ellie had a predilection for risk-taking – a fact that hadn't gone unnoticed, by many of the teachers, over the years. Jake was hidden somewhere in the undergrowth, and Ellie had just finished counting backwards from ten. As soon as she had finished counting and had opened her eyes, she plunged through the bracken in pursuit. Stray twigs and thorns tore fresh holes in her cardigan as she went. Ellie cared little for her clothes, and as the result of previous explorations, her jeans bore holes in the knee and, similarly, her trainers – holes in the toe.

Mr Harrison was standing at the office doorway. His smile was courteous and refined. In his right hand, he held a small bag of soft mints. Mrs Atkinson waved him in, distractedly. 'Stanley,' she said. 'By all means, come in. Forgive me, I was in a world of my own.'

The deputy head entered and placed the mints on the desk. 'The door was open, so I…' He faltered.

'Quite.' She returned his smile with a fleeting one of her own, one that just tinged the corners of her mouth with the merest ascent before vanishing again.

Mr Harrison settled himself into a chair and opened the bag of mints with a small pop. 'My sister sent me some sweets,' he explained. 'It's, erm… it's my birthday today.'

'Oh, Stanley,' said Mrs Atkinson apologetically. 'Of course it is. All these years, and I quite forgot.' She ran her fingers through her long, jet-black hair, pushing it away from her face. 'I'm sorry.' He waved away her apologies, dropped a mint into his mouth and offered her the bag. Mrs Atkinson at first hesitated, then took one, reclining in her seat and sucking thoughtfully.

Ellie had ducked. She was crouching low to the ground, like a tiger waiting to spring. She was deaf, and in order to make the game as even-handed as possible, Jake wore a school tie around his head to cover his ears. She could already see him; his tie was jutting out like bunny ears. She giggled. He was a good sport but rubbish at hiding.

She rose carefully and edged nearer, feeling the twigs beneath her feet snap as she went. When she was within a couple of feet, she dropped back down to the earthen floor, watching him as he peered out from his hiding place. She shook her head. She had always been far better at this game than him. She waited a moment longer, watching the bunny ears flit about as he looked vainly from side to side. She counted backwards in her head. *Three... two... one.* Then she sprang up from her patch of foliage, making a grab for his back. He moved away just in time, but his tie had become dislodged.

Strictly speaking, she had found him and therefore, the game should have been over, but neither one of them would have it end there.

Mr Harrison's eyes made a cursory sweep of the office interior, as he sat, sucking in silence.

'By the way,' he said, his voice thick with saliva. 'Have you heard anything of our great protector?'

'Not for months.' Mrs Atkinson rolled her eyes.

'Silence is...'

'Disturbing,' she finished.

He bowed his head and touched his hands together as though in prayer. 'I suppose they'll be in touch once term starts.'

'I suppose.'

'But of course, with such an influx of students coming to us now from the St. Jude's disaster,' he continued, 'it can't help but make one wonder.'

'I know,' Mrs Atkinson said, with a grim expression on her face. 'Believe me, Stanley, I know.' She was very tired, and as her glance wandered from Mr Harrison to her desktop, it rested there on a small-framed picture of her, with a man and two small children. 'But what use is wondering? We've always known it is too late for our generation, but for the youngsters...' She stopped herself by putting a hand over her mouth. Mr Harrison was unsure whether her expression bore one of revulsion for the mint she had swallowed too soon or because she had almost allowed her darkest fears to leave her lips. She straightened her back. 'You don't have children, do you, Stanley?'

Tradition would generally have their game develop into a mad chase through the forest. Neither Ellie nor Jake would really consider the game to be over until one of them was pinned to the floor and ready to submit. She picked up the tie that had fallen to the ground and sniffed at it as though she were on the trail of its scent.

Jake tore through the forest ahead of her. He could run faster than her, no question, but Ellie was a master strategist. She grinned to herself, then darted off in a different direction to the one he had taken. She knew that instinct would ultimately lead him to their treehouse. They had built the house in that particular tree precisely because it was their favourite in the forest. It was not only tall but grand. Its trunk was so vast, and gave rise to so many further branches, it was as though the tree were pushing the surrounding trees out of its way. It had extended itself a slight clearing around the base but grew quickly up into a mass of leaves and branches. Jake and Ellie's house was constructed so far towards the top of the tree that it was quite invisible from ground level. It was to this tree that Ellie now ran.

She climbed up to the first level of branches with well-honed precision. The light was definitely fading from the sky with greater haste than this time last week and she shivered a little under the breeze. She settled on one of the lower-lying branches and brought her knees up to her chin, hugging her tattered cardigan around her legs as she waited.

Mr Harrison had just popped another mint into his mouth. 'What's on your mind, Yvette?'

Mrs Atkinson sat still for another moment, then leaned forward in her seat. Her words shot out like rapid fire. 'I feel the flight-to-freedom programme is in jeopardy. Our protector has been too silent in his communications – ominously silent. His actions, I'm afraid, to coin an old-fashioned term, are speaking far louder than his words.'

Mr Harrison swallowed and dabbed the corners of his mouth with a sleeve. 'What do you mean, "in jeopardy"?'

Ellie caught sight of Jake moving stealthily through the surrounding undergrowth. He was moving with caution, as though he knew the tree might possibly be guarded. She watched as he crouched low and inched himself closer to the trunk, doing her best not to laugh.

Glancing over his shoulders all the while, Jake skipped the last few steps and placed a hand against the tree, as though it were a checkpoint he had reached and where he might now be safe. Ellie looked down at him as he wandered around the base in semi-circular patterns. He paused directly beneath her feet. Unable to resist, Ellie extended the arm that was still holding his school tie and let it slip from her fingers.

Jake watched the tie fall before his eyes in momentary bewilderment. Then, in the split second it took for his brain to join up the dots, Ellie had landed on him from above. She pinned his arms down into the soil, her knees clamped tightly around his waist. He fought in vain to topple her, but she was in too strong a position. She laughed manically as he struggled again.

'OK, OK, OK,' he said.

Mrs Atkinson had risen from her chair and was looking out of her office window. She stared out at the darkening sky and rested her hands upon the sill. 'There'd be nothing we could do about it,' she said. 'They could cut the programme at any time.'

Mr Harrison attempted a reassuring chuckle that rang slightly hollow. 'They can't just cut the programme.'

Mrs Atkinson turned on him, her arms folded tightly across her chest. 'I think you'd be surprised just what the Legion is capable of.' Then she threw up her hands with an air of indifference. 'I'm sorry, Stanley. You come here on your birthday for a chat and all you get is scaremongering.'

'It's fine,' he said quietly.

Mrs Atkinson's expression took on a faraway quality, and she looked back outside. 'All we can do is play our part,' she said, more to herself. 'We must aim for a one hundred per cent pass rate in this year's Level Twelves.'

'One hundred per cent?' asked Mr Harrison doubtfully.

She turned upon him a face of solemn determination. 'And one hundred per cent next year,' she said.

Jake had known Ellie since their very first year together in Oakham. He had managed to learn some sign language, and this was generally how they communicated with one another; but since his arms were currently pinned to the ground, he was forced to speak.

Ellie moved her face closer to his so as to make out what he was saying through the dusk.

'Enough, enough!'

Ellie continued to hold him down, throwing her head back and laughing hysterically. He knew the rules as well as her: only a full admission of defeat would do.

'OK, *OK*,' he said grudgingly. She inspected his lips again and waited for the magic words. 'You win,' he said. 'I give up.' She relaxed her arms and allowed herself to sink down upon his chest, which was heaving with exhaustion. They looked at each other for a moment longer in satisfied silence, then she allowed herself to roll off him and they both lay on their backs, looking up into the mass of branches.

In that moment, when Ellie sank down upon his chest and it crossed Jake's mind that she might be about to kiss him for the very first time, Mrs Atkinson was leaving her office, with Mr Harrison in tow. She locked the door behind them and they made their way along the corridor. 'If you would like to continue this discussion, I suggest we walk and talk. I have to do my dormitory checks.'

Mr Harrison stuffed the remaining mints into an inside pocket of his jacket. 'Why don't you let me do the checks for a change?' he said. 'You could have an evening off if you like.'

'Thank you, Stanley,' she said. 'But it is not out of an overdeveloped sense of school duty that I do these checks. It is not term time yet. No.' She paused. 'I do these additional checks for my own peace of mind and, as such, it would be quite out of the question to expect someone else to perform them on my behalf.' She smiled at him. 'But thanks all the same.'

Ellie and Jake, meanwhile, had climbed to sit at the top of their tree. The sky above them glistened with stars as the final veils of night were being drawn, and the two young friends knew that they would soon have to be back in their beds.

Jake pointed to a star that was far larger and brighter than the rest. 'What do you suppose that one is?' he said. Ellie sat leaning on her elbows. She looked up at the star and shrugged without interest. Jake jabbed her in the ribs and said, 'Don't you think it's beautiful?' Ellie smiled a slow, deliberate smile and shook her head. Jake muttered something as he turned away from her, and Ellie had to hit him to remind him to face her when speaking. 'I said I think it is,' he said defensively.

Ellie nodded slowly. Then she composed a question for him in sign. 'Why is it so much brighter than all the rest?'

'That's just the way it is,' said Jake with the air of a man of the world. 'I suppose no two stars are the same, just like people. Some shine brighter than others.'

Ellie nodded, then signed, 'Maybe some are just further away than others.'

'Come on,' said Jake, obviously slightly nettled. 'It's getting late. We ought to get back before Atkinson checks in on us.'

They slipped and slid their way down the trunk of the tree until they landed with muffled thuds on the leafy ground. Without pausing, Jake flung his tie loosely over his head and strode off in the direction of the school gate.

Ellie had to run to catch him up. She hadn't meant to hurt his feelings, but he was funny when he got, what she called, 'sentimental about things'. He strode out, his face a set frown. Into an unoccupied hand that swung carelessly at his side crept Ellie's. Jake was, at first, taken aback. He looked at her, surprised, but she only returned his gaze with an unfathomable smile. Of all the school students, she was the most curious and perplexing, and it was for that reason Jake had always been so drawn to her. He offered a small smile in return as they neared the school perimeter fence. One at a time they ducked under a purpose-built hole at the base and, with the ease of great practise, scurried across the tarmac within.

They hoisted themselves through a kitchen window, the same small window that they always used. The kitchen opened onto a small canteen that was only ever used by staff, and beyond that was the grand main hall. From here it was relatively straightforward to get back upstairs and on towards the dormitories. However, the building was ancient and they would have to clamber up three flights of stairs before they parted ways.

When finally, they reached the top, Jake gave Ellie's hand a gentle squeeze.

'Be careful,' he signed. 'Atkinson will be on patrol. We're late.'

Ellie nodded, squeezed back in farewell and watched him disappear down the corridor to the boys' common room. Between her and the girls' sleeping quarters, there was one final adjoining corridor to her right. She started out towards it, but as she approached the intersection, she caught sight of Mrs Atkinson and Mr Harrison walking up the connecting corridor towards her. They appeared to be deep in conversation, however, and hadn't yet seen her. Ellie withdrew at once and pressed herself up against the near wall. She wouldn't be able to stay there for long. If the teachers reached the junction and turned left, they would be upon her. If they reached the junction and turned right, they would reach her dormitory before her and surely see that she was not in bed.

She had to pass them, and she had to do it now. Every moment that she hesitated, the more likely she was to get caught. She peered carefully around the corner. They were now talking so earnestly that she felt she should be able to cross the corridor without them seeing her, but no sooner had this thought occurred, both teachers looked up again. She pulled back sharply, swallowed a deep breath and peeped round once more. Neither teacher was speaking now and both were looking dead ahead as they walked. Ellie would have to wait until one of them spoke. Surely then they would turn to face each other again and she would have a split-second window to make her move. She pressed herself as flat as she could against the wall, waiting for her chance.

They were getting dangerously close. Ellie had to concentrate hard on her breathing and control her rising panic. She shrank as far as she could into the shadow, hugging the wall while still keeping an eye on them.

It was Mr Harrison who spoke first. Ellie saw his pace slacken suddenly, as though a thought had crossed his mind, and her heart gave a flutter of anticipation. She stared at him until his lips began to move and watched as his mouth began to form a question. Knowing that Mrs Atkinson was bound to shift her gaze to him at any second, she gathered herself to run for it. She watched Mr Harrison say, 'So, if the flight-to-freedom programme were to be cut this year...' Mrs Atkinson's mouth opened to engage, but in that moment, Ellie was gone.

She dashed straight across their path and towards her dormitory door on the other side. She had no idea whether she had been seen or not, but she could not stop to find out. She must just make it to her bed. If she had been spotted, she would soon know about it. She slipped open the bedroom door, where nine other girls already lay fast asleep. Tiptoeing over to her bottom bunk, she slipped noiselessly under her sheets, drawing them up to her chin so that her outer clothes would not be visible upon inspection.

In what seemed like only a matter of seconds later, the door was opened again and Mrs Atkinson stood silhouetted in the frame. Through the bedroom window, the light from Jake's brilliant star cast a cold glow across the floor to Ellie's bed. What with that and the light that came in from the door, she felt as though she were under a spotlight. She lay with her eyelids determinedly clamped shut, trying to breathe naturally, and waited for the stern hand of officialdom to land on her shoulder and hoick her out of bed, but it never did. After what seemed like an eternity, Ellie sensed the light subside and knew that the door had been closed. She opened her eyes slowly and stared through the window. Jake's star now seemed almost as big as the moon.

As she gazed critically up at it, a puzzlement began to form in her mind. What on Earth had Mr Harrison been saying? She played it back: 'If the flight-to-freedom programme were to be cut this year...' *What on Earth would make him suggest such a thing?*

T W O

As ELLIE LAY in bed, she thought back over Mr Harrison's words. She played the sentence over and over in her mind, trying to apply logic in the vain hope that reason would conquer doubt and ultimately she would feel that there was nothing whatsoever to worry about. Rational thinking, however, became more difficult to achieve with every attempt. Her eyelids felt as though they were becoming heavier every time she replayed the movement of Mr Harrison's lips. Before long the lips were all she could see. Her understanding of the words became obscured by fatigue, until eventually physical exhaustion won out and she slipped unshakably into a deep and dreamless sleep.

She came around the following morning, still feeling weary. Her eyes were foggy as she blinked up at the ceiling. The other girls were already awake. They were either sitting around chatting or had already up and gone. Ellie rubbed her eyes with the back of her hand. She looked around, catching single words or phrases, but was too tired to really grasp any coherent conversation. She pulled back her sheets and swung her legs out of the bed, revealing the same torn, bedraggled jeans and cardigan of the night before. She hadn't even taken her trainers off. She sighed inwardly, feeling the conversations falter and the looks of the other girls follow her across the room. She had always had a knack for drawing attention to herself. She flung the dormitory door open, with a low moan.

The corridor outside was draughty. Instinctively, she hunched her shoulders against the chill. Other students were already filling the hallways. Some walked around with puffy eyes and toothbrushes sticking out of their mouths, others were dressed and making their way down to the main hall for breakfast. Ellie decided to follow the procession going downstairs and head straight to the dining hall. She looked around, still bleary-eyed, and fell into step behind a group of girls whose hair shone with brilliance and bounced in long, lustrous waves around their small heads as they bobbed along the corridor. Their socks were pulled up to above their knees, and they radiated energy and eagerness. *First years*, thought Ellie. She wrapped her arms around her waist as she followed, spotting an old toothpaste stain on the hem of her sleeve as she did so.

The train of students led to a noticeboard just outside the main hall and they congregated there. Ellie craned her neck to see what everyone was looking at. There was a large message stating that an equipment list had been issued for the start of term and beneath, separate notices for the different year groups. Further down, each student had a tailored list to meet their own specific requirements. Ellie found her year group and scanned the list for her name. According to the document, she needed a new stylus for her work pad. *That's true.* She had tried to use the last one as a makeshift antenna to pick up radio signals with an antique device she had found in the forest. She had fried the stylus and broken the radio. Her cheeks reddened slightly at the memory of it. She also needed new clothes, a new bag and something called a 'Speaking Aid'. She sighed. There would be busses into the city today, every hour, on the hour. All trips would have to be supervised by an adult. There was another notice about the St. Jude's School disaster, but Ellie didn't stop to read it. She was hungry.

'What do you have on your list, then?'

Jake had appeared by her side. He looked similarly tired, as he studied the noticeboard, searching for his own name. 'Oh,' he said brightly, 'mine's not too bad. I need a new... tie,' he read aloud. Ellie avoided his eye and guiltily studied the floor. She couldn't help but feel partially responsible for the heavy-handed treatment that some of his possessions had been subjected to. His tie was certainly among these items. A mental flashback of the thing being thrown to the ground and trodden into the mud during one of their play fights flashed across her mind. Her eyes widened as she motioned that they should go into the main hall.

Together they walked up and down the magnificent aisles of food troughs, grabbing at piles of bacon and scrambled eggs. Ellie loved the smell of bacon and she built hers into an impressive pyramid on her plate. Jake placed a slice of toast in his mouth, which he held between his teeth as he tried to make more room on his plate for mushrooms and hash browns. Ellie looked at him and laughed, her gesture indicating, 'Don't you think you have enough?' Jake, who could interpret most of her expressions by now, returned it with a sarcastic laugh, emitting a dust cloud of toasted breadcrumbs as he did so. 'Yeah, yeah, yeah.'

They sat down on a pew near to the rest of their peer group and attacked their bacon as though it had been days since their last meal.

'So, come on,' said Jake thickly, through a mouthful of scrambled eggs, 'have you got much shopping to do?'

She nodded grimly.

'What do you need?'

Ellie made the sign for, 'Everything,' then pinched a mushroom from his plate.

'That sucks,' he said, watching her thieving hand in mock outrage. 'I probably won't go in until the afternoon. I've got football this morning, plus I don't need much. I'll probably just…' He stopped. Ellie's attention had drifted. She was no longer following what he was saying. 'Hey,' said Jake. 'Sorry, am I boring you?'

'Sorry,' she signed.

'What's up?'

Ellie hesitated, then began to describe to him the close call she had had with Mrs Atkinson and Mr Harrison the night before. She explained how she had made it to her bed only seconds before the door was opened and the room inspected.

Jake's face contorted as he used his tongue to inspect something that had become wedged between two of his back teeth. 'We need to be more careful,' he said at last. 'This year of all years, we really ought to be more careful.'

Ellie pinched another one of his mushrooms. 'There's something else.'

'What is it?'

Carefully, she relayed exactly what she had seen Mr Harrison say.

'Why would they cut the programme?' Jake countered. 'It doesn't make any sense.'

Ellie shrugged and Jake frowned thoughtfully at his eggs. Then his face cleared. 'He was probably saying something like, "If the flight-to-freedom programme were to be cut this year..." would apes take over the planet?' He laughed at his own joke, then stabbed at another rasher of bacon with his fork; but Ellie looked less convinced.

'What if it's more serious?'

'We don't know that—'

'But—'

Jake interrupted her hands and looked at her closely. 'We can't get into thinking, *What if,*' he said. 'Where's that gonna get us? One way or another, we'll find out if the programme changes.'

Ellie freed her hands. 'Should we just *ask* them?'

'No,' said Jake quickly. 'Are you insane? You don't want them to know you were out after curfew. Besides, if they scrap the programme, they will have to tell us anyway.'

'So what do we do?'

'Just wait.'

Ellie looked at him doubtfully and Jake knew full well just how incredibly difficult she would find it to 'just wait' in reality. She loved solving puzzles and mysteries.

'Don't do anything, Ellie,' he said knowingly. 'Don't do anything that will expose our rule-breaking.'

Ellie nodded for his sake and told herself that he was probably right. It was probably nothing.

After breakfast, she went back to her room to pack a bag for the shopping expedition. She would try to get a morning bus to the city and get the whole thing over with. She would start the term properly and play her part well. She would be a dutiful and dedicated student. She would work hard and pass her Level Twelves. She would also keep half an eye out for answers to the question of what Mr Harrison had been talking about. *There would be no harm in that.* She shoved layers of clothing at random into her old school bag. The seams of her bag were splitting, and she would certainly need a new one; she merely resented the noticeboard for having recognised this fact before she had.

By the time Ellie had made it back downstairs for the 10am bus, she could see Jake doing laps of the neighbouring field with the football team. She felt funny about not being with him for the journey, and a little nervous about navigating the city alone. Still, she never wanted to have to rely on anybody else for anything, and with that in mind, she swallowed her misgivings and marched out to join the queue.

The line for the bus was slow-moving and by the time she was boarding, space inside was fairly limited. She managed eventually to find a seat right at the back, next to a harassed-looking boy with a distinct skin complaint. She smiled politely as she perched next to him and he returned her smile with a feeble one of his own, scratching behind his ears. When the last of the students were seated, two teachers in long black robes boarded the bus before the doors slid shut.

As the bus moved jerkily into gear, Ellie's eyes wandered over the other groups of students. A couple of the girls from her year sat across from her. Ellie recognised Sienna and Tess, though she had never had any dealings with them. They appeared to be talking excitedly about their post-exam life.

'When I get to the safe station,' Sienna was saying, 'I'm going to go into tourism. It's an industry that has been absolutely destroyed here on Earth.'

Tess said that she thought that sounded very interesting indeed. 'I hear tourism is absolutely thriving there.'

'Of course it is,' said Sienna. 'I suppose it's like having a new planet to discover. It's like having Earth again, only with a failsafe.'

They laughed haughtily. Then they spotted Ellie watching them and they returned her stare with proud, arrogant ones. 'Can we help you?' said Sienna.

Ellie shook her head.

'What's the matter?' said Tess. 'Can't you talk?'

Ellie shook her head again and shrugged.

'Oh my God, she actually can't,' said Sienna. Then they huddled together with such furtiveness for a few minutes, covering their mouths partially with their hands as they did so that Ellie could no longer keep up. She sighed and leaned back in her seat. A moment later, she received a jab in the arm, and when she looked, the girls were staring at her as though she were an exhibit in a zoo.

'We were just talking about our futures after the Level Twelves; you know, when we join the Legion,' explained Sienna. 'But don't worry, it probably doesn't concern you. Your future is most likely going to be here.' She gestured out of the window towards passing wasteland and landfill sites.

Ellie frowned, then said in sign, 'What makes you say that?'

Sienna regarded Ellie's hands with an expression of abhorrence. 'Sorry,' she said. 'We don't speak *loser*.'

Ellie felt a movement in the seat next to her. Both Sienna and Tess looked from Ellie to the boy sat next to her. They each pulled faces of the deepest disgust and returned quietly to their original conversation. Ellie turned to the boy, curious to know what had been said. He slowly, but capably, put together a sentence with his fingers.

'I just told them what I thought you'd asked.'

'You know sign language?'

'A little,' signalled the boy. 'My mother used it in her work.'

'What does she do?' asked Ellie.

His chin dropped a fraction before he answered, 'She's dead.'

'Sorry.'

Ellie wondered whether to offer that she believed her parents to be dead as well but decided not to, as the truth of the matter was that their bodies had never been discovered, and Ellie still held on to the tiniest of hopes that they might one day return to her.

The boy bowed his head, and for a moment neither one of them spoke.

'What's your name?' he said at last.

'Ellie.'

'Hi, Ellie,' said the boy politely. 'I'm Jasper.'

'Are you nervous about the Level Twelves, Jasper?'

The boy sniffed and scratched at an inflammation on the side of his neck. 'I know I'm not going to pass, but I'm not worried about it.'

Ellie looked at him with indignation. 'What do you mean?'

Jasper sighed. 'The Legion has built a superior planet to this one. It is supposed to be a planet where disease and infection no longer exist.' He pulled back his sleeve to reveal the broken and irritated skin that ran all the way up his arms. 'Do you really think they'll let *me* in?'

Ellie hit him playfully on the arm for reassurance, but Jasper's expression remained stony.

'Seriously?'

'Let's just say I have my doubts,' he said.

Ellie flushed. 'But if you pass your exams, they'll have to take you.'

'*Have to?*' He laughed. 'They're building their own race. They can do whatever they want.'

Ellie's face was swathed in confusion, but she shook herself out of it long enough to compose another question. 'Wouldn't it scare you to stay behind?'

'Not really,' said Jasper. 'Better the devil you know. Besides, I don't trust Le Dich.'

'Who?'

'Leader of the Legion,' said Jasper. 'I'm a strong believer that if something sounds too good to be true, it usually is.'

Ellie was struggling against a feeling of nausea from the pit of her stomach, which manifested itself in some regurgitated bile in her mouth. Her shoulders gave a reflex spasm. She sat for a moment, slightly hunched, feeling foolish. This Jasper appeared to have his finger on the pulse of current affairs to such an extent that it had totally exposed her gaping ignorance. She sat back in her seat and swallowed the bile, her face pallid. Noticing her ashen expression, Jasper hastily changed his tack. 'Hey, maybe I'm wrong about the Legion,' he said. 'It's just one guy's opinion, after all.'

Ellie looked at him. She could tell that he was not being sincere. He didn't really believe that he could be wrong. He went to speak again, but she raised a hand to signal that the conversation was over. She rested her head back and closed her eyes, waiting patiently for the journey to end.

As Ellie queued to exit the bus, she looked out of the window and remembered making the same journey the previous year, but even then, only a year earlier, the foetidness of the situation on Earth had not been quite so apparent as it was now. As they filed out this time, they were each issued with a facemask, a bus timetable and a vaccination jab. Their names were checked on a list and they were given an emergency tracking device, which they had to wear around their wrists at all times.

Sienna and Tess received their jabs with elaborate praise for each other's bravery. They looked back at Ellie as they fixed their facemasks and disappeared into the grey urban wilds. Jasper sped off alone as soon as his feet touched the ground and Ellie didn't see him again until the return journey to Oakham. She spent her time in the city, shopping alone. She peered out from her facemask as she moved between the tall, imposing buildings. The streets were awash with people. There were people lying down and huddled in doorways. There were people rummaging through refuse units. Even through her mask, the stench of the place was unbearable, and she desperately hoped against hope that she would not pick up an infection.

She walked as fast as she could between the shops, using her school credit card to purchase her bag, uniform and general clothes. She did not stay long in the clothes shops. They bored her immensely. Besides, the items she was buying were essential items, not luxury ones. There was nothing personal about the shopping expedition.

Gloomily, she scanned her equipment list, fixed on the last item, and set off in the direction of Gadget

Planet. Her spirits, however, rose when she found the shop. The entrance was small, but there was an energy emanating from within. Hastily, she made her way to the door, which slid open to admit her with an automated swoosh.

Ellie's eyes gleamed as she stood in the foyer and gazed around at the vast interior. There were miniature rockets racing each other in figures of eight in and around the high cavernous ceiling. Great imposing robot arms moved and rotated to operate lift functions to upper levels of the shop. Ellie was staring around at the jiving mannequins with such rapt attention that she did not at first notice the store clerk who had appeared next to her and was now asking her if she needed any assistance. With a holographic hand, the clerk waved in front of Ellie's face playfully. Ellie started and looked at the light projection with interest. It was of a boy of about seventeen, who was now saying for the second time, 'Can I help you with anything today?' Ellie blinked, trying to recall the purpose of her visit. Then, with renewed clarity, she began to rummage in her pocket. Her hands seized on her equipment list and she pulled it up, showing the boy triumphantly her required 'Speaking Aid'. She held it up to his face proudly, as though it were her golden ticket, and her reason for being there was now completely justified.

Comprehension spread over the clerk's face. 'Follow me,' he said. Ellie followed excitedly as the clerk lead her to a counter towards the back of the shop. The image of his moving form flickered sporadically as she kept pace with him. Reaching the counter, he turned to her and indicated rows and rows of tiny white boxes. He studied the labels, then stood back, pointing towards one of the boxes, with triumph. 'There you go,' he said. Ellie picked the box up and turned it over in her hands. She couldn't help but feel slightly disappointed. The shop was so big and dynamic, yet the item she had been sent to pick out, for school, was so small and inconsequential that it sat comfortably in the palm of her hand. Ellie considered bitterly that it must have been the most boring of all the items in the shop. She smiled at the clerk, as best she could, scanned the item against the censor and swiped her card carelessly. She shoved the 'Speaking Aid' deep into her bag and immediately forgot all about it.

As she walked back through the swooshing doors of Gadget Planet, it took a moment for Ellie to reacclimatise. In her hesitation, a dishevelled-looking man in a long, dark overcoat loomed out at her from a shadowy archway. Ellie jumped back so fast that she did not see what the man was asking. The only phrase she glimpsed on his lips was, 'Please, miss.' With her heart threatening to burst out of her chest, she ran in the direction of the bus stop.

Although she and Jasper returned on the same bus, they did not sit together. Ellie sat down first this time and she watched Jasper move straight past her and sit next to another boy, at the back of the bus. She didn't care. She was tired and dirty.

She spoke to no one on the journey home. Instead, she closed her eyes and tried to conjure happy thoughts, but the city had been in a far greater state of decay than

Ellie could have imagined. She sat in the bus, letting the motion rock her gently from side to side. She considered whether she would rather live here on this Earth after her Level Twelves or on a new planet governed by the supreme leader Jasper had mentioned. She knew nothing of this Le Dich, and it occurred to her that she only had the word of the school that the 'safe station' was all that it was cracked up to be, the same school that was now potentially going to shut down the flight-to-freedom programme altogether. It proved a difficult choice to make, and she still hadn't made it when the bus stopped outside the main entrance hall of the school. She still hadn't made it when she had tramped up the three flights of stairs to her dormitory door. She pushed the door open with her shoulder, shopping bags hanging from her hands and wrists.

She let them fall to the carpet as she gazed around the room in wonder. The layout of the room had been altered. It took a moment for Ellie to understand what had happened. More beds had been crammed in. There was little space left to manoeuvre and she kicked her fallen bags petulantly over, towards her bunk.

A girl Ellie had never seen before sat cross-legged on the top. She had dark brown hair like Ellie, but unlike Ellie's, which would only just reach to tuck behind her ears, hers was long and wavy. It hung down, obscuring part of her face, and the eye that was visible through the folds regarded Ellie with a look of deep misgiving. Ellie paused for a moment, looking at the eye, wondering if this curious spectacle was going to say anything. She watched carefully for a moment, but the girl never appeared to move her mouth. Ellie was relieved. She was too tired, anyway; she didn't know why her dormitory had gone from being a ten-person room to a twenty-person room since she had left it, and just at that particular moment, she didn't care. She collapsed onto her bed in a heap and kicked off her trainers with a contemptuous attitude.

THREE

'MUM?' ELLIE LOOKED around, disbelieving. She noticed that she was standing in a fairground. The woman looked like her mother, but she did not acknowledge or even look at her. She looked straight through Ellie to a carousel, holding an infant child in her arms. Ellie turned to watch the carousel as it rotated slowly, round and round. Plastic horses were jiving up and down, wearing fixed painted grins on their faces. Slowly the music began to play. She could *hear* it. She could hear the carnival-style music emanating from the carousel's speaker. Then she could hear other children laughing. She turned back to her mother in time to see a man running over to them. The man was balancing three ice creams in his hands and grinning from ear to ear. 'Here you are,' he said. He handed Ellie's mother an ice cream. 'And here's one for you, Ellie, darling,' he went on. 'Your very first ice cream.'

Ellie stared from her mother to her father and lastly at her infant self. She watched the child critically as it struggled to hold the ice cream in its tiny hands. It managed to smear the melted delight all around its mouth in clumsy deliriousness. Ellie turned away in disgust. She could hear the sound of people's voices all around. She tried again to speak to her mother. 'Mum!' she shouted; but it was no use. Ellie placed a hand to her throat. She could feel the vibration of her vocal cords and she tried again – 'Mum, Mum!' – but no sound came from her. She could hear everything but herself.

She looked desperately around at the other families, but no one seemed to be able to see her, even. In a gesture of hopelessness, she sank to the ground and passed her hands over the tops of the grass. It felt warm from the sun, and she ran her fingers back and forth through the blades. The breeze was gentle, and she craned her neck back to look up at the sky. Far away in the distance, the sky was beginning to turn from the deep blue of a cloudless summer. Pale clouds were gathering and churning into thick, dark, stormy ones. Ellie jumped to her feet with a jolt of panic. She knew how quickly the weather could change from one extreme to another. She had cause to know. She looked wildly around for the nearest wind shelter hub, but there was nothing there. She looked at her parents. They were still eating their ice creams and watching the carousel. Ellie looked at the other families, but everyone seemed ignorant of the threat that was gathering pace overhead and streaking out towards them.

Ellie ran to her mother and grabbed her by the arms desperately. 'Move it,' she tried to say. 'Run!' But again, her voice never made it out of her, and her mother continued to look through her as though she were not even there. As the sky cracked and the storm started crashing around them, fresh gusts tore at the ground like pitchforks. Ellie let her hands slip from her mother's arms. She *wasn't* there. Ellie didn't know if it was an accurate memory, but she did now know that she had to be dreaming. She had never known what had happened to her parents, and as the wind kicked the grass and debris high up into the air, Ellie stared unflinchingly at them, waiting for a clue. The couple stood static as the storm surged around them, as though they were not in the least bit aware of it. Ellie could see them gazing at one another, laughing idiotically.

The storm raged harder, but the family stood their ground, quite unfazed. Ellie began to hear another sound. It was the sound of someone crying. She squinted through the howling wind at the infant 'her', but baby Ellie was not the one crying. Baby Ellie, moreover, seemed just as blissfully unaware of the destruction being dealt by the storm as her adoring parents. Still, the crying continued. She looked around for the owner of the voice. She swung her head from side to side so furiously, as she looked, that she did in fact shake herself awake.

When she opened her eyes, she was staring blankly through the darkness of her dormitory to the bunk above her. It took a moment or two for Ellie to remember exactly where she was, and what was real. Although she had had the carousel dream before, it always took her a moment to recover from it.

She lay in the darkness, sweat standing out on her forehead, taking deep breaths. She shivered a little as the sweat turned cold and trickled down the sides of her face. She climbed wearily out of bed, her eyes adjusting to the dark as she went. Groping, with outstretched arms, she found her way to the dormitory door and pushed it carefully open, stepping lightly out into the corridor and making her way down the hall to the bathroom.

The light in the girls' bathroom was startlingly bright in contrast to the dormitory. Ellie rubbed the corners of her eyes and opened the cold tap. She cupped her hands under the cool running water and sloshed it over her face in soothing pools. She looked at herself in the mirror and bared her teeth. She had a near-faultless set but for one on the bottom row that sat a little behind the rest and appeared, as a result, forever slightly discoloured. She stood inspecting them in absent-minded wonder when a movement from behind her reflection caused her to jump. A cubicle door swung open. She spun around and came face to face with a girl that she recognised immediately as her new bunkmate. She remembered having seen the girl with the long wavy hair just before she had gone to bed. The girl had stared at her through her thick folds of hair and not said a word. The girl now stared at her again, only this time Ellie could see that her cheeks were red and tears were running down them in steady streams. The girl's chest heaved and she said unhappily, 'What are you doing here?'

Ellie stared back at the girl in silence, wondering how to respond. The slight hesitation seemed to madden the girl and she took a step closer. 'I said, what are you doing here?' Ellie backed up a touch but could already feel the porcelain sink behind her, trapping her. 'So,' surmised the girl, 'you heard someone crying, and thought, what? That you would just come out here and stick your nose in?'

Ellie did not like the way the girl appeared to be speaking to her, but she thought back to her dream. She *had* heard someone crying. *But it couldn't have been real; it was a dream.* The girl took another step forward, pushing Ellie back until she was almost sitting in the sink. Enough was enough, and Ellie pushed the girl sharply in the chest, surprising both of them. The girl stumbled backwards into the cubicle door. For a second, she was too taken aback to react, and it was while she was reeling from this that Ellie hastened to explain. She made the sign for, 'I'm deaf.' The girl faltered, again caught off guard. 'I'm deaf, so I couldn't have heard you crying, *understand*?' Ellie folded her arms defensively and glared at her angrily.

The girl looked back at Ellie with mingled curiosity and suspicion. She could interpret roughly what Ellie had said, but she still did not look entirely convinced. 'What are you doing out of bed?'

Ellie shrugged overtly and signalled, 'What are *you* doing out of bed?' Again, this was easy enough for the girl to interpret. She also liked Ellie's brashness. She understood that Ellie was telling the truth; there was no way she could have heard her. She also appreciated the hostility, displayed. It was an emotion that she could readily identify with, and she felt that Ellie had been quite within her rights to have pushed her.

'Who are you?' she said slowly. Ellie wrote her name in the bathroom mirror. There was not a huge amount of condensation in the room, but the smudges her fingers made left enough of an impression for the girl to make it out. 'Ellie?' she clarified. Ellie nodded and pointed to the girl expectantly. 'I'm Dana,' said the girl. 'I just transferred here from St. Jude's.' She lowered long, attractive lashes over her flushed and dampened cheeks. She sniffed. 'Our school was flooded. The water broke the barriers and we had to be airlifted to safety. The number of students who survived is apparently just a little over half, and now,' she flapped her arms in a gesture of hopelessness, 'now we are here. Didn't you see the notice about it?'

Ellie hesitated, feeling for sure that this did ring a vague bell. She fidgeted with her hands, thinking about what she would say next.

'Wait,' said Dana, taking a mini work pad and stylus from her back pocket. 'I write in this,' she said. 'I write everything in here. It's like my diary, I guess. If I open up a new document, you can write to me. I can talk and you can, you know... write.' She offered Ellie the work pad. Ellie dithered for a moment, then took it.

'Why couldn't you sleep?' prompted Dana.

Ellie scrawled over the work pad with the stylus, and then held it up for Dana to see. She had written, 'I had a bad dream.'

Dana nodded. 'Uh huh, what about?' Dana's stare was intense, as it fixed on Ellie, through the hair curtains.

It was the sort of stare that would force the truth out of anybody, Ellie considered.

'It's a recurring nightmare, about my parents,' she wrote.

'OK,' said Dana thoughtfully. 'What do you think brought that on?' Ellie shrugged automatically, but Dana looked at her sideways and said, 'Come on.' Ellie hunched over the work pad and set to work. It was, in fact, therapeutic to write it all down. She explained to Dana the disconcerting conversation she had had with Jasper about the Legion and how he had inferred that Legion selection could come down to anything other than exam results. She relayed the snippet of conversation she had witnessed between Mr Harrison and Mrs Atkinson about the flight-to-freedom programme and how Jake had convinced her not to follow up these concerns for fear of landing themselves in more trouble. She wrote at length, admitting that something inside her had a bad feeling and how it must have been this bad feeling that had brought about the dream. When she finally returned the work pad, Dana had to read for several minutes before she could respond.

When she did respond, she pulled out an old locket from around her neck. She opened it up for Ellie to see. 'It was my mother's,' she said quietly. There were two pictures inside. One was unmistakably a picture of Dana herself. The other was of another girl, who looked a little bit like her, only older and with straighter hair. Ellie looked from one to the other.

'That's my sister,' said Dana. 'She'd be fifteen this year. Three years ago she took her Level Twelves. She passed, too. She's incredibly smart.' Dana studied her fingernails briefly and gave a little sigh. 'I have to believe that she is on that safe station, Ellie. I have to believe that she made it. She worked so hard to get there.'

Ellie scribbled furiously over her work pad. 'Why wouldn't she be?'

Dana swallowed. 'I was in the audience at her graduation,' she said. 'There were Legion reps there, too. They called her name, but she never appeared. They called it again. Everyone was looking around for her, but still she didn't come.' She paused, and Ellie shrugged at her, encouraging her to explain what had happened next. 'Well,' said Dana, 'then they just moved on to the next name on the list.'

Ellie frowned in consternation. She started to write and got as far as, 'But wh—' before Dana put a hand over the pad to stop her. 'My sister has juvenile Parkinsonism,' she explained. Ellie looked at her blankly. 'It's like Parkinson's disease in teenagers,' Dana said. 'Now, I'm not sure exactly what or who to believe, but if this Jasper is on to something, then it may be that my sister never joined the flight-to-freedom. If she had a disease and the Legion is trying to be disease-free...' She closed her eyes. 'I have to know, Ellie. One way or another, I have to find out.'

Ellie nodded in understanding. 'I will help you find out,' she signed.

Dana flashed a broad smile and wiped away her tears. 'Thank you,' she said.

Ellie motioned that they should go and Dana nodded in silent assent. They walked side by side back to the dormitory. As they approached the door, however, Ellie walked straight past it. 'Hey,' said Dana, 'where are you going?'

Ellie handed her the work pad and gestured for Dana to go back to bed. 'Ellie!' Dana hissed. 'What are you up to?'

'There's someone else we need, on side.'

Dana could not interpret this, and Ellie knew it. She gave an, 'I'll tell you later,' wave of her hand and strode purposefully down the hallway. She proceeded straight across to the boys' sleeping quarters. Dana slipped back into her own room, creeping nervously through the dark and unfamiliar confines. Ellie was gently prising open the door to the boys' common room. Inside, there were further doors to separate dorms. Ellie knew which one Jake was in; they had sneaked out together enough times over the years. Carefully, she opened the door to 'dorm six' and crept inside.

The room smelled of sleep and body odour. Ellie pulled a face in the dark and covered her nose with a sleeve. Just as in her room, this dorm had been reshuffled to accommodate more beds. She knew that if Jake had had any say in the matter, his bed would be next to the window. He liked to look at the stars. Silently, she crept to the bed nearest the window. Sure enough, there he was. Unlike her, he preferred the top bunk, so Ellie would have to climb up to him.

She put a foot in the first rung of the ladder, just inches from another boy's nose. As she hoisted herself up to the next rung, she felt the ladder vibrate slightly beneath her feet. She imagined it must be creaking. She was too far along to stop now, so she climbed up another rung. Again, she felt the metal beneath her feet vibrate and shudder. She could almost reach Jake now. She wondered how best to wake him, making the least possible noise. She opted for placing a hand over his mouth. She stood on her toes and reached out to his face, bringing her hand down over his mouth in a firm grip. There was a split second before Jake started to have the sensation that he was drowning. He was startled violently out of his sleep, his moans muffled by the grip Ellie held tightly over his mouth and nose. He stared at her in startled confusion, recovering himself just in time to grab her, pull her up from the ladder and under the sheets before the dormitory light was switched on. Everybody was awake, and all the boys were looking over at Jake's bunk. 'Sorry,' he announced to the room. 'I had a nightmare. I'm alright now. Sorry.' Disgruntled and embittered comments were voiced.

Jake was clamping his sheets down conspicuously around him and the boys were looking at him with mingled curiosity and trepidation. His face was emblazoned with guilt, but he offered no further explanation and ultimately weariness won the battle over intrigue. Slowly all heads returned to their pillows and the light was eventually switched off.

Jake lifted his sheet and peered underneath. Ellie had her mouth covered but looked as though she was on the verge of wetting herself with mirth. He had to wait a fairly long time before he heard the sound of collective heavy breathing, but when he thought it was safe enough, he climbed down the ladder of his bunk, with Ellie close behind. He led the way back out into the common room, where he turned on her angrily. 'I thought we agreed we were going to be more careful,' he mouthed. His face was white with fear. 'Tomorrow is the first day of term. This year is the big one, Ellie. What are you sneaking around for?'

Ellie stroked his arm soothingly until his wrath had reduced to a simmer and his breathing levelled out. She relayed the story of her encounter with Dana in the bathroom.

'I'm really sorry for this girl and her sister, but what can *we* do?'

'We can investigate it.'

'How?'

'I don't know,' motioned Ellie forlornly. 'I don't have it all figured out, but she needs a friend. Maybe we can start with that.'

'You came to tell me you want me to be a friend to some girl you've just met?'

Ellie nodded.

'This is all very well,' whispered Jake, rubbing his eyes with the palm of his hands, 'but couldn't it have waited 'til the morning?'

'Where's the fun in that?' Ellie smiled.

'Excuse me?'

'I wouldn't have got to see you in your lovely pyjamas,' she teased, poking him in the belly.

'Stop that,' he almost yelled. 'You're crazy, you know that?'

Ellie regained control of her expression. 'She is scared,' she signed. 'She is scared that the programme might have failed her sister. I'm scared that the programme might be about to fail us. Help us?'

'Fine,' said Jake, 'but I don't think anything's going to fail anyone.'

'I hope you're right.' She wrapped her arms around his middle and held him like a comforter.

'Trust me,' he whispered, his ears glowing like the lights on a runway.

FOUR

THE MAIN HALL was alive with the clamour of excited voices. The students were finding their seats for the first assembly of the year. Representatives of every department stood at the front of the hall on a raised platform, waiting for silence. Mr Harrison was patrolling up and down the rows of students, performing postural analysis and confiscating bags of smuggled-in chocolate and jumping beans. He glanced towards the stage and bit his lip. *Where is she?*

Mrs Atkinson was standing over a desk that was located in a small staff room bordering the main hall. She was hunched over a work pad, scrolling through a document and nibbling her stylus. She looked up as Mr Everton, the Level Nine leader, entered with Mr Harrison close behind. 'Good morning, Yvette,' said Mr Everton. 'Are we ready to go?'

Mrs Atkinson grimaced. 'Not quite,' she said. 'Is everybody here?'

'The staff are waiting,' Mr Harrison replied.

'Good,' said Mrs Atkinson, straightening her back. 'Bring them in here, would you?'

They both stared at her in amazement, and Mr Harrison continued, 'Erm… the students are taking their seats, Yvette. We're ready for you to start.'

'I understand,' said Mrs Atkinson, smiling patiently. 'Still, show the staff in here, would you? The students will have to wait.' Mr Harrison tried to disguise his irritation and hastily motioned for Mr Everton to carry out the instruction. Mr Everton stalled for another moment, then ducked outside to relay the message. He walked over to the line of teachers and Level Leaders that stood at the front of the hall. He approached the first teacher, Mrs Ulsworthy. As he whispered in her ear, her face creased a little in surprise and apprehension. She looked back at Mr Everton as though to make quite sure she had heard him correctly. He nodded encouragingly before moving on to the next teacher. As Mr Everton went all the way down the line, the teachers began slowly to move off, out of position and towards the staff-room door. Interested murmurs from the student collective followed their uneasy departure. Ellie, Dana and Jake exchanged a bewildered look.

Ellie was sitting in her new uniform. She fidgeted with the hem of her skirt and pulled her socks up for the third time that morning. When she looked at the other girls around her, she noticed that no one else seemed to suffer the same affliction of perpetually sinking knee-lengths. Jake sat on one side of her, his back straight and arms folded. On the other side of her sat Dana, who placed a hand on top of Ellie's. Ellie wondered if this was to comfort her or an attempt to keep her from fidgeting.

'I'm sorry to have called you all in here like this,' said Mrs Atkinson as her confused members of staff packed into the tiny office. 'I hope you all know that I wouldn't call you away unless I had a good reason.' Murmurs of agreement. 'As some of you are aware, communications with the Legion have halted of late. There has been no word from Le Dich regarding the flight-to-freedom programme, and, more precisely, its funding. Indeed, we haven't heard from him since the beginning of July.' Grumbles of disillusionment, tutting and much sighing ensued. 'No word, that is…' Mrs Atkinson raised her voice a notch and waited for the hubbub to abate, 'until this morning.' She placed her palms down on the desk and studied her congregation. Silence fell. Mrs Atkinson paused, then said, 'The flight-to-freedom programme is to be abolished as of next year.' The roar of discontent that followed was audible to the waiting mass of students in the outside hall. Ellie felt the bodies bristle around her. Students who had been chatting and idly playing about in the wake of the adults' departure now sat stock-still. Everyone was looking at the door through which the staff had vanished. Ellie looked at Jake, who shrugged, his arms still clasped firmly round his middle.

Mrs Atkinson had the ability to speak in a voice that carried to the far end of a room, either by projecting it loudly or by reducing it to a low and steady monotone. It was with the latter projection that she now addressed her team. 'The reason for this cut has not yet been given,' she said. 'I would not like to speculate as to the reason, and I strongly suggest that you too resist that temptation. I wanted you to all know as much as I do, and now you do. Please keep any theories at this stage to yourselves. We will not break the news to our students, until we know of a resolution.' She stopped. Then as an afterthought, she said, 'If anyone would like to ask a question, I will do my best to answer it, but please try and keep it brief; we do still have an assembly to conduct, after all.'

There was silence, broken eventually by the small and high-pitched squeak of Mrs Ulsworthy. 'If it is a matter of money, might we try a fundraising exercise to extend the programme?'

'We might,' conceded Mrs Atkinson. 'That is a very positive suggestion, Eileen. Thank you.' She looked around the room of troubled brows. 'Anybody else?' No one spoke. 'Right,' she said with an ironic arc of her eyebrows. 'Let's do this.'

Ellie watched the teachers carefully as they made their way back onto the stage. They had not exactly been the picture of merriment before the interruption, but now there was something different in their expressions – something more sinister. She turned to Dana, who seemed to be thinking similar thoughts. 'Something's wrong,' she mouthed.

Mrs Atkinson was the last to enter the hall. She stepped up onto the stage and addressed the crowd with a clarity similar to the chime of an antique clock. There was not the slightest hint of interference from the audience. Everybody looked at her. 'I am sorry to have kept you all waiting.' She beamed. 'Every year is challenging at Oakham. It is challenging because it is important, and the most important things in life don't always come easy. As ever, you will all have to work extremely hard. We have known for a long time now, what we stand to gain through hard work.' She turned her delivery towards Ellie's peer group. 'For those of you taking your Level Twelves this year, I wish you all the very best of luck.' She coughed discreetly behind a raised fist. 'To those of you joining us for the first time, I welcome you. This year we have students joining us at all levels of the school. This is due in particular to the disastrous floods that have affected St. Jude's School. I sincerely hope that those of you who have come to us from St. Jude's will enjoy your time here and that those of you who are returning to us for another year will make yourselves known to the new students.'

Mrs Atkinson skipped through some of the standard points regarding absence formalities, school boundaries and the corporal punishment that would come falling down upon the head of anybody who didn't pay heed to them. There was laughter from the audience, but Mrs Atkinson said, 'I'm not even joking.' Laughter again, but less buoyant. She waited again for silence, and when she had it, she went on to introduce each member of staff individually.

They were all dressed in smart suits. The more senior members of staff and the Level Leaders sported black robes with gold trim. There was one member of staff, however, who did not quite conform to type. He wore navy-blue trousers, with pockets all the way up the legs, large work boots with metal toes, a torn beige sweatshirt and a utility belt. The way he stood was also different. Most teachers stood straight, with their hands clasped neatly in front of them. This man stood, slightly hunched, with his hands thrust into his pockets. Long lank hair cascaded down the back of his neck, and his beard grew into a point, extending his chin and giving him something akin to a lion's mane. Small, circular glasses perched on the end of his nose and Ellie stared at him in fascination. She didn't recall ever having seen him before, and when he stepped forward, she paid particular attention to what Mrs Atkinson would say about him.

'Mr Francis joins us this year from St. Jude's. He will be involved in field trips and city excursions, as well as heading a new voluntary metal works department. Those of you who are interested in metal works and construction, please add your name to his list, on the noticeboard. You will have to use a pen, mind you, as Mr Francis works with paper,' she shot a smile over to the metal works master, 'as well as many other interesting antiques, I'm sure.'

'Well, I am an antique myself,' said Mr Francis. There was a titter of appreciation from the audience. It was only the second voice to have spoken during the whole assembly. It was out of turn and Mrs Atkinson was as surprised as anyone. To some, it displayed a reassuring level of good humour; to others, it was the height of bad manners. Though the students were immediately divided in their assessment of him, Mrs Atkinson, who recovered before anyone else, wore a set and entirely enigmatic expression. Ellie grinned; she liked antiques.

Ellie was still grinning when they all left the main hall and were heading to their first class. Dana rounded on her. 'What's up with you? What's so funny?'

Ellie shook her head. *Nothing.*

'Well, they didn't spend very long talking about the Level Twelves, did they? Just, "Work hard," and, "Best of luck." Well, obviously!' Dana pouted her lips. 'I mean, didn't anyone else find that just a little bit strange?'

'Not really,' said Jake. 'What else are they going to say?'

'How about some success stories?' countered Dana. 'We never see anything of the people who have joined the programme. We are never even shown the safe station. For all we know, it's hideous! How about giving us some incentive to do well?'

'Do you really need more of an incentive after what you've been through?' asked Jake. 'Anyway, if it's a choice between this and the unknown, I'll take the unknown.'

'That doesn't surprise me,' said Dana. 'I guess people like you are pretty much only interested in the next big thrill.'

'What do you mean, "people like me"?'

'You know,' said Dana, 'simple, with short attention spans.'

Jake's face was beetroot red. He puffed his chest and drew breath to reply, but Ellie intervened, touching both of them gently on the arm. They looked at her, expecting a further gesture of appeasement, but she stopped just long enough to shake her head and give them each a look of disapproval. Her eyes then glazed over and she began moving off again in a trance-like state of hypnosis. Dana and Jake looked at each other, both bemused, then hastened after her.

She was thinking about Mr Francis. His appearance, demeanour and apparent total self-assuredness had completely bewitched her, and as the three of them sat down to their first class of the day, neither Jake nor Dana could coax any further communications from her.

'Good morning, good morning, good morning,' sang out Mr Adlington as he swept into the classroom, brandishing a bag of pebbles and a packet of Jelly Babies. 'If you're present, please say "aye".'

Twenty-six students chorused, 'Aye!'

'If you're not here, please say "nay",' said Mr Adlington, removing his jacket and placing it on the back of his chair.

'Nay,' said one boy from the corner of the room.

'Since you have answered both "aye" and "nay", Mr Jennings, I can only assume you are neither here nor there.' Mr Adlington raised one eyebrow in theatrical concern and sucked in his bottom lip. There was an appreciative snicker from around the room.

'Moving on,' said Mr Adlington. 'Who can tell me what these are?' He held aloft the bag of black pebbles. 'Mr Reeve?'

Matthew Reeve announced rather smugly that the pebbles were mini projectors, called *Pablucto Silvantes*, and that they could project images up to one hundred times their size. 'They are a bit limited, in that you can't use moving images, but—'

'Thank you, Mr Reeve,' interrupted Mr Adlington. 'I'm sure they will do for the purposes of my display. OK, I am going to hand out a dozen projectors. I want you to hold them tight, and not turn them on until I say. How many projectors am I going to hand out?'

'A dozen,' came the collective response.

'Right you are,' said Mr Adlington before turning back to Luke Jennings. 'You know how many that is, don't you, Mr Jennings? That means twelve.' The boy grimaced at the witticism. 'OK,' said Mr Adlington. 'Start catching!'

He threw projectors into parts of the room. One of them hit Ellie in the chest as she sat at her desk, resting her chin in her hands and looking out of the window. 'Wake up, Miss Webster,' called Mr Adlington. Ellie, roused from her thoughts, looked round to see what had happened. Mr Adlington held eye contact with her, and mouthed, 'Wake up,' again, silently and just for her.

Ellie had always liked Mr Adlington. He was one of the few teachers who could use sign language, and his energy was infectious. She grinned at him, back in the room.

'OK, Ellie. You're going to go first,' he said. 'On the count of three, press the white button on your pebble. Aim it anywhere in the room. Ready? One… two… three…'

Ellie pressed the button and a beam of light shot out of the end of the pebble. She directed it towards the ceiling, and the whole class peered up at it. The image depicted what looked like the piece of a jigsaw puzzle, only the edges of the piece were rough and jagged. 'OK,' said Mr Adlington. 'What do we think *that* is?'

'It's a piece of cheese,' someone called out.

'Not even close,' said the teacher.

'Scrap metal?' came another suggestion.

'One more try?'

'It looks like some kind of landmass,' said Jake.

'Very good, Mr Wilks,' said Mr Adlington. 'Can anyone tell me which bit of land it is?' Jake squinted up at the projection, uncertain.

'It's the Lake District,' said Dana.

Mr Adlington clicked his fingers and pointed at Dana with eyes bright. 'It is!' he said. 'It is indeed the Lake District; or, to be more precise, it is the Lake District today.' He returned to his bag. 'I have another dozen pebbles here. A dozen; that's how many, Mr Jennings?'

'Twelve,' said Luke Jennings reluctantly.

'I'm glad to see you have settled on being here, Mr Jennings, and not elsewhere.' He looked at Dana again. 'I don't know who you are; who are you?'

'Dana.'

'Dana?'

'Humphries.'

'Very good, Miss Humphries. I am now going to pass you another pebble and the same rules apply: don't press the button until I say. Are you ready to catch?'

'Yes,' said Dana.

'OK, one… two… three, catch.'

Mr Adlington threw the pebble. Dana caught it with both hands above her head and waited. 'OK, Miss Humphries; when you're ready, press that button.'

Dana pressed down and another beam of light shot up to the ceiling, which she steadied and positioned next to Ellie's.

'Now then,' said Mr Adlington. 'What is *that*, do we think?' No one spoke. 'Come on,' he said. 'Isn't anyone going to have a guess?'

'It just looks like a different landmass; a smaller one,' said somebody.

'What if I told you that it is still the Lake District, and that the maps are to the same scale?'

'I'd say you were crazy,' said Luke Jennings.

'Hmm,' agreed Mr Adlington. 'It may be crazy, Mr Jennings, but I assure you it is true.' He addressed the whole room. 'How can that be?'

'It's the future,' said Jake.

Mr Adlington smiled in deep satisfaction. 'It is a projection of the Lake District one hundred years from now,' he said, giving Jake a thumbs-up. 'Mr Wilks, you may have just earned yourself a Jelly Baby.'

The class then set about revealing the ten remaining landmasses, which depicted other regions of the UK. They then had to work together to assemble and complete the map, making a true representation of the United Kingdom. Having done so, they then had to repeat the process with the twelve projectors of the forecasted map of Britain.

As the students pieced together their maps, Mr Adlington made his way around the room, inspecting the progress. When he got to Ellie's desk, he stopped and crouched down. 'Is everything OK?' he signed.

Ellie nodded. 'Is this outcome set? Is there no way we can stop this from happening?'

'There is nothing *we* can do,' Mr Adlington signed. 'But nature can do whatever it wants. Nature is full of surprises, so not all hope is lost. OK?'

Ellie nodded but felt far from OK. 'Seems like a bit of a gamble.'

Mr Adlington rose back up from her desk and spoke. 'Faith,' he said cryptically, 'perhaps the biggest gamble of them all.'

When the class had ended, Ellie, Jake and Dana walked out into the hallway and in the direction of the student common room. There would be a short break before the next class, during which Jake had said he'd like to get a sandwich.

'How can you eat now?' said Dana. 'Did that class not affect you in the slightest?'

'Well, it didn't put me off my appetite, if that's what you mean?'

'Obviously,' said Dana. 'I can't belie…' She stopped. They both looked at Ellie, who had carried on walking straight past the common room door and in the direction of the main hall. They followed her until she stopped outside the hall and stood, staring up at the noticeboard.

'What are you doing?' Jake asked her.

Ellie looked at them both as though she had only just noticed that they were there. She used sign language to say to Jake, 'I'm signing up for the metal works classes.'

'What?' said Jake.

'What is it?' said Dana. 'What did she say?'

Jake sighed. He knew that when Ellie set her mind to something, there was very little chance of her not seeing it through. Any protestation on his part would be pointless at this stage. He looked at Dana.

'Do you have a pen?'

FIVE

THE END OF the first day of term came not a moment too soon for Ellie. The final class of the day was a history lesson, which had concentrated heavily on rock and roll music, and the influence it had had on the world, particularly during the mid- to late-twentieth century. It did not help that Ellie found this subject monumentally boring. She enjoyed reading about the antique devices that had been used to transmit the music, but she had no interest in fashions and trends. Still, she noted down the key dates and terms and strived to pay attention until the very final minute.

The end of class was signalled by a loud alarm that linked wirelessly to a bracelet on Ellie's arm. As the bracelet buzzed happily, she slipped her work pad and stylus back into her bag with a puff of her cheeks. She was tired, but she still wanted to go to the treehouse. She followed the line of students that snaked into the corridor and waited there for Jake and Dana to appear. History was a mandatory subject, and since the whole year group had to sit it during the same hour of the day, the class was taught in several different rooms, by several different teachers. As fate would have it, Ellie had been separated from her friends for the last and most tedious subject of the day. She rocked back and forth on the balls of her feet while she waited.

When they emerged, both Jake and Dana looked pensive and drained. Ellie wondered if they had spent the afternoon bickering. For one reason or another, Jake and Dana did not seem to have hit it off quite as naturally as she had hoped. She raised her hand to them as they approached and smiled hesitantly.

'Shall we go?' said Jake.

Ellie nodded, then indicated that Jake should extend the invite.

'Right,' he said, looking at Dana. 'We're going to the forest. Do you want to come with us?'

Dana gaped at them, apprehension and excitement both melded in her expression. 'But, the forest is off-limits,' she said. 'Remember what Atkinson said, this morning?'

'Ellie and I have been going there forever,' said Jake dismissively. 'Don't worry, it's perfectly safe.'

'You rebels,' she mocked.

Ellie nodded encouragingly, but Dana shook her head. 'Thank you, but no. I want to have a shower, anyway, and write my diary.'

Ellie gave a thumbs-down and mouthed, 'Boring.'

'Maybe another time?' Jake said.

'Sure,' said Dana with the smallest hint of a smile. 'Maybe.'

Ellie clapped Dana encouragingly on the shoulder in farewell and looked at Jake with let's-get-out-of-here eyes. Jake went to follow her, making apologetic see-you-later gestures to Dana as he did so. He followed Ellie's already disappearing form as it bounced around a bend in the corridor towards the main hall. When he got to the bend, she was already through the doors and into the staff canteen beyond.

He ran to catch her up, reaching the canteen just as she was approaching the far kitchen window. Ellie slipped through the partition easily, but in his hurry to keep up, Jake scrambled through the window, stumbling as he dropped down to the ground outside. He landed hard on his knees and scraped the palms of his hands along the outside wall. He was bruised and looked annoyed as he studied his grazes. Ellie laughed and grabbed at the neck of his sweater, trying to pull him to his feet. 'Come on,' she waved impatiently, before dashing off again to the hole in the fence.

'I thought you said that girl wanted to be friends,' said Jake when the two of them sat together at the top of the tree, five minutes later – Ellie making annotations in her planner and Jake nursing the cuts on his hands.

'She does.'

'With you, maybe. She doesn't seem to want to be mine.'

'She's just new. You have to make an effort.'

'I am,' said Jake defensively. He looked at her as she scrolled through the pages of her planner. 'What are you doing?'

'I'm entering the dates of my metal works classes.'

'Why did you sign up to that?' asked Jake, sucking his hand. 'It's completely voluntary, you know; as in, it doesn't count towards your final grade.'

'I know,' signed Ellie with half a shrug.

'You're crazy, you are.'

Ellie contorted her features into a wild grin. 'Yeah, I'm crazy. I wanted to learn something just for fun.'

'You'll be signing up for the field trips next.'

Ellie looked down and supressed a giggle.

Jake placed a hand to his head. 'Seriously?' he said. 'You didn't think you might have enough on your plate this year?'

'It's in the *Peak District*.'

'So?'

'So, I've never been there.'

Jake scoffed. 'You'll have to be vaccinated, you know.'

'I know.'

'I'm just saying, it's not like it's gonna be a holiday.'

'No,' conceded Ellie. 'It is supposed to be an *educational* trip. Besides,' she smiled, 'what would I be doing otherwise?'

'How about studying for your Level Twelves? You can learn all about the Peak District without having to go there.'

'I *want* to go there.'

'It's dangerous, Ellie.' Jake face was suddenly serious, and he stretched out a hand to take hers. 'Look at what happened to your parents.'

Ellie flinched, taken aback. He had never mentioned her parents before, and it had caught her off guard. She fixed him with a poker-faced stare and pulled her hand away and out of reaching distance. 'That happened when I was a baby,' she signed.

'And it's worse now,' said Jake.

Ellie looked at him. 'Exactly.' She widened her eyes, for emphasis. 'When *I* get to the safe station, I want to be able to teach others about where we came from; don't you? Hands-on experience is so much more authentic, don't you think?'

'Why would you want to teach people about our mistakes?'

Ellie shook her head at him sadly. 'If we don't learn from our mistakes, what is there to prevent us from making them again?'

Jake licked his hand and stared blankly out to the sky. 'Whatever,' he said. Ellie punched him on the arm to remind him to face her when speaking.

'What did you say?'

'Nothing.'

'If you think the trip is a waste of time, don't come.'

'I won't,' he said.

'Fine.'

'Fine.'

'Good. Me and Dana will go on our own.'

'Dana's going?'

Ellie nodded and flung her work pad back into her bag. She pulled the straps over her shoulders.

'Where are you going now?'

'To my induction.'

'Alright. I'll leave with you then,' said Jake.

'Up to you.' She shrugged.

She was feeling saddened by his attitude. She had thought that the three of them would enjoy the field trip. She was surprised at his concern for the health-and-safety aspect, too, considering they sneaked out of the school most nights to sit in a restricted area of forest. She also felt disappointed at his lack of effort with Dana. She had taken it for granted that he would have welcomed her and the challenge of finding out what had happened to her sister. His ambivalence towards the matter niggled Ellie. She suspected that Jake would not really be able to stay behind from the trip, when it came to it. *He was bluffing, but why? There's something up with him*, she considered; but right now she didn't care to think about it. She was feeling excited about her evening class and she didn't want to let anything ruin that.

As they climbed back through the kitchen window into the staff canteen, Ellie knew she was at least half an hour early, but she strode purposefully towards the main hall, leaving Jake to make his own way back upstairs.

When she reached the main hall, she stopped in front of a map of the building. The map was labelled with sections of the school that Ellie had never visited in all the time she had been there. She was thrilled to see that the newly labelled wood and metal works department was located in one such section. It had a whole basement floor to itself. She traced a finger over the map and mentally assimilated with a tingle of anticipation that the main workshop was situated directly below her feet. Ellie hastened over to the lifts, pressed the 'call' button and waited. As the light of the button changed from red to green and the doors pulled jerkily apart, she stepped over the threshold, her tummy playing host to a band of butterflies.

She scanned the numbers and dials on the inside of the lift, eventually spotting a button marked 'Basement'. Feeling thrilled at the very idea of it, she pushed the button and waited for the doors to close. There was a small pause before anything happened, a false start and then suddenly the lift began to plummet to the depths of the building's foundations. It fell through the shaft as though it had quite come adrift from its mechanism.

The compartment felt as though it were in free-fall and Ellie's butterflies were propelled to the roof of her mouth. She thought for a minute that she was going to be sick. She grabbed at a handrail to steady herself, her hair flicking up around her head and stretching towards the roof of the cubicle. Panic rose from inside when she imagined that the lift might actually be broken. She closed her eyes at the thought of the force she was liable to meet the ground with.

The lift plunged further down, the g-force of the propulsion now remodelling Ellie's cheeks. She was just considering that there must be a hole in the bottom of the school, through which she was now hurtling towards the centre of the Earth, when suddenly the lift skidded to a jarring halt.

Ellie stood for a moment and waited for gravity to reclaim its hold on her. She tucked her hair back behind her ears and opened one eye cautiously. She took one tentative step forward before the lift gave a final unexpected lurch. The doors flew back, and Ellie was deposited onto the floor of the outside corridor with a resounding cough. With great dignity, she picked herself up from the floor and dusted off her knees and elbows. She looked back at the lift dubiously. The lift replied by snapping its doors shut behind her, like the jaws of a gnashing wolf. Ellie took a few deep calming breaths and tried to recover what was left of her nervous system; then she turned around to inspect the dark corridor before which she now stood.

She inched forward. The corridor was short and opened up into a large, cavernous chamber ahead of her. The cave was so dark that she was blinking blindly for several minutes before her eyes had adjusted sufficiently to it. There appeared to be several further tunnels and passageways jutting off from the cave. She carefully made her way over to the first tunnel on her right and groped the wall until she found a label. Pulling her stylus from her bag, she touched the nib with her thumb and a small light shone from the end. She aimed this at the label and faintly made out the word 'cafeteria'. Frowning, she moved around to the next tunnel and searched again with her tiny torch. She located a sign this time that read 'WC'. She exhaled deeply and moved on. As she circled the cave, the next tunnel was labelled 'Storage', the one after that 'Wood Workshop' and the one after that 'Metal Workshop'. She looked over her shoulder and considered that she had nearly come full circle. She hovered uncertainly between the passageways before finding the inscription 'Office', which defined the last tunnel. It was through this tunnel that Ellie decided to go.

The corridor that followed was narrow and smelled of damp. Ellie shivered as something dripped from the ceiling, caught her on the back of the neck and trickled down her spine. She was starting to doubt the wisdom of having arrived quite so early for the class. The corridor was longer than she had anticipated, and as she walked, fresh doubts flashed across her mind. What if this was not the right floor after all? What if she had passed way beyond the school to some underground commune of giant moles? What if the moles fed on human interlopers?

She shook her head, telling herself not to be such a baby. When dim lights began to emanate from an opening at the end of the tunnel, she slackened her pace more still and peered around furtively. She stepped up to the opening on the tips of her toes and peeped out into what looked like a doctor's waiting room. It was a very small room, but there were a couple of chairs set down outside of a wooden door. On the door a crude engraving read the name Mr Francis. Ellie sighed with relief and knocked on the door. She waited for a moment, but the door was not immediately opened. It was still early. She sat down on one of the wooden chairs, restlessly re-tucked her hair behind her ears and waited.

As it happened, Mr Francis was in and had heard the knock at the door. 'Come in,' he had murmured. He was scrolling through his work pad, browsing online auctions for second-hand tools and other odds and ends. He was deeply involved in searching for the best possible deals. 'Hello?' he called again. There was no reply. He groaned inwardly, tearing himself away from the screen and shuffling around piles of bric-a-brac to answer the door.

A girl sat outside. She was perched on one of his new chairs. 'Hello,' he said again. The girl did not speak. Instead she raised a hand and smiled. Mr Francis was, for a moment, at a loss. 'Won't you come in?' he said at last. Ellie nodded, rose from her seat and followed him into the office.

She stood by the door, fiddling with the hem of her skirt as Mr Francis cleared a small area in front of his desk for her to sit at. The office was littered with strange artefacts, most of which Ellie could not identify. He shoved everything to one side and gestured for her to sit down. He noticed her studying an ancient coffee grinder, which sat on an old filing cabinet behind his desk, a metal arm protruding from it wildly. He moved over to the object, smiling from one corner of his mouth. He popped the lid open and showed Ellie the inside theatrically, like a magician at a children's birthday party. Ellie watched expectantly. He then brought forth a handful of coffee beans from another container and placed them inside the grinder. 'Then for the fun part,' he said, turning the metal arm in wide circles. He paused after a time and reached back inside the grinder, showing Ellie the freshly ground coffee. 'Would you like a cup?' Ellie grinned and nodded.

Mr Francis silently worked away at preparing the coffee, wondering how next to address this strange child. He poured out two mugs of sludgy brown liquid and handed one to Ellie, who sniffed at the mug discreetly as Mr Francis slumped back into his chair. He gulped from his own mug, while Ellie took a tentative sip and winced, her shoulders inching up to around her ears. It was very hot. She blew into it, took a deeper gulp and felt the liquid coursing through her body. It enlivened the senses in her chest and arms. It reached the tips of her fingers with a slight tingle. The second taste had been better. She smiled in satisfaction and saw that Mr Francis was chuckling. 'It does grow on you,' he said. He placed his own mug down on the desk and pushed his small round glasses back up the bridge of his nose. 'What is your name?'

Ellie placed her mug on the desk and tapped the fingers of her right hand to her left. Comprehension dawned on Mr Francis's face. 'You'll have to forgive my ignorance, but I don't know what you just said.' He leaned forward in his seat. 'Have you got a Speaking Aid?' Ellie stared at him, wondering what on Earth he was talking about. Then she remembered the thing that she had been sent to Gadget Planet to buy from her Level Twelve itinerary list. She rummaged in her bag, pulling out a small plastic package. She handed it to Mr Francis, who turned it over, inspecting it quizzically. He then began to wrestle it open with strong, blunt fingers. After a few moments he brought forth a length of material. It looked like a cloth necklace of some kind, with a sapphire-blue emblem in the middle. There was also what looked like a small blue microchip. It was crescent moon-shaped, and Mr Francis held it up to the light.

'Right,' he said. 'This goes in your ear, apparently.' He held the delicate device out to Ellie, who assessed it with scepticism. 'Go on,' he said. Ellie took the chip and placed it inside her ear, where it rested loosely, before slipping and guiding its own way right down the canal to her inner ear. She jolted at the sensation, but Mr Francis smiled and glanced again at the packet instructions. 'Is it all the way in there?' he said. Ellie nodded. 'Right,' he said. 'Now, this ties round the neck.' He handed her the cloth necklace, which she took and fastened. She manoeuvred the blue emblem until it rested at the front. It was a snug fit, but the material was soft and she liked it aesthetically. 'The Speaking Aid is supposed to interpret your thoughts and voice them,' went on Mr Francis. 'According to these instructions, it works with vibrations. You should feel the speech through the choker.' Ellie stared at him in unconcealed amazement. 'Shall we give it a go?' he said. Ellie nodded slowly. 'OK,' said Mr Francis. 'What is your name?'

A deep male American accent emitted from the sapphire emblem. 'Ellie,' it said. Mr Francis laughed and Ellie frowned, not understanding the joke. He caught himself and said, 'Just give me a minute to adjust the settings.' He took back the contraption and muttered to himself as he sat hunched over the instruction manual. 'There you go,' he said finally, handing the necklace back to her. 'Now you should sound like a girl of twelve, and not a man of forty.'

Ellie smiled, catching up on what had happened. 'How about now?'

'Much better,' said Mr Francis. 'Now, Ellie, what can I do for you?'

SIX

For the next fifteen minutes Mr Francis listened while Ellie experimented with her new Speaking Aid. She gave him the run-through of her entire day, starting with how she had signed up for his class immediately after the assembly. She described how she had been able to concentrate on little else during her other classes, and how this had resulted in her being hit by a hurled pebble projector. Finally, she relayed to him the disturbing experience she had had in the lift. 'I have been meaning to fix that,' he said. 'But honestly, Ellie, there has been so much to do since I arrived. The place was completely filled with junk. You should've seen it.' Ellie cast an eye over Mr Francis's office and wondered just where his definition of 'filled with junk' differed from other people's.

Mr Francis rose from his chair and drained the last of his coffee. 'What is it?' said Ellie.

'It sounds as though there are a few more people arriving,' he explained. He looked at her critically. 'Does the earpiece not heighten your sense of hearing, as well?'

Ellie shook her head. 'No,' she said. 'I didn't think it would. My hearing loss is called *Sensori-neural*. It comes from a head injury I had when I was a baby. It is permanent and hearing aids don't help.'

'I'm sorry,' said Mr Francis, 'but you can speak?'

Ellie stood and picked up her school bag. 'Theoretically,' she said. 'Anyway, I can now.'

When they reached the large central cave, Mr Francis flicked a switch on the wall and rows of large strip lights sprang into life above their heads, one by one. The ceiling of the cave was extremely high up, and large dehumidifiers hung suspended from rafters. Ellie noticed that all of the other students appeared to be boys. They chatted together excitedly, though some looked mildly queasy, following their ride in the lift. They were all squinting around as their eyes adjusted to the light. It wasn't a large group, Ellie considered. There were about sixteen students all told, and the first thing Mr Francis did was to ask everybody to stand in a circle.

The group shuffled into a ring, surrounding Mr Francis, who stood in the middle, surveying them all until the chatter had virtually ceased. He gave a brief and perfunctory welcome to the class, emphasising how much he was looking forward to getting to know them all, before moving hastily on to having the class introduce themselves one at a time. He asked them to give their names, to supply an interesting fact about themselves as well as an example of something they were hoping to achieve from taking the class. When Ellie's turn came, she explained that her name was Ellie, that she was deaf and needed people to face her when speaking. She also said that she was looking forward to handling power tools. This met with an appreciative chuckle from the rest of the group and she scanned the watching faces as they welcomed her warmly and in unison. 'Hi, Ellie.'

Mr Francis then divided the group into four smaller groups. He gave each group a box and in each box was something that needed constructing. 'Your projects are for you and your group only,' he said as they each stood before their boxes, hovering as though they were waiting for a whistle before diving in. 'You and your three team members are going to work together to construct whatever it is you have in front of you. Don't think about what the other groups are doing at this stage. I want you to concentrate on working together in your groups. Later on we will see how we can work together as a whole unit.'

The class murmured with excitement. Ellie's group fell to their knees and began at once to pull out large pieces of metal hinges and bolts. They chatted together animatedly, all eager to perform better than the other groups. As they set about their tasks, however, it dawned on them all just how difficult the class may end up being. Ellie grimaced in horror as she turned over bits and parts that she could not liken to anything she had seen in the instruction booklet. The others in her group were looking equally perplexed. They shot discreet glances around the room, to assess how well the other groups were getting on, but everyone was looking just as confused as them.

'What do you think of Francis?' said one of the boys, picking up a bag of turbo bolts and holding them up to the light.

'Seems OK,' said another.

'There's no image for what we're building,' moaned the third boy, as he inspected the booklet. 'There's a list of parts with pictures, but no image of the final piece. How are we supposed to know what we're aiming for?'

'We're not supposed to know,' came Ellie's electronic response. 'It's designed to keep us working strictly to each instruction so that we follow it properly and don't make any assumptions.'

Two of the boys exchanged *you-can't-be-serious* looks, but the first boy was looking at Ellie. He studied her with piercing blue eyes, shaded beneath dark, prominent eyebrows. They gave his face, Ellie considered, a movie-star charisma, which she happened to find eminently pleasing.

'Ellie, right?'

'That's right.'

The boy extended a hand, which Ellie shook in return. 'I'm Harvey,' he said.

The boy who had been poring over the instruction booklet looked up. 'Oh, I'm Doug,' he said.

'Nick,' said the other.

Harvey addressed the group with authority, placing his hands on his hips as he spoke. 'Well, gang,' he said. 'I think Ellie is right. We're gonna have our work cut out for us here. We'll have to approach this methodically. Let's spread out the parts so that we can clearly see what we've got in front of us. Then we'll look at part one and separate out what we need for that. We won't even think about any of the other parts until we get on to part two; agreed?'

Nick and Doug looked at each other, then at Harvey. 'If you say so.'

'Unless anyone has a better idea,' said Harvey, his glance resting on Ellie.

'No,' said Ellie. 'That's good.'

'Great.'

The group resumed their task with slightly less enthusiasm than before, though they worked steadily through the pile of bits for the next half an hour in relative silence, making sure that they had all the pieces necessary for 'part one'. As more bits and pieces were removed from the box, so their occupied area of floor space grew outwards.

At one point, Mr Francis passed by their industriously working huddle. He stopped and grinned down at them. 'Wow,' he said. 'I have to hand it to you, that's quite a mess.'

'We're just accounting for everything,' explained Harvey.

'Oh, so there is method in the madness? I am relieved.' He flashed a wink at Ellie and moved on to the next group.

During the final twenty minutes of the class, Ellie, Harvey, Nick and Doug decided that they had all the parts they needed to begin. They managed to screw some runners into a metal panel and loosely map out where other panels were liable to adjoin the first, when Mr Francis called for them to stop what they were doing.

There was a collective groan while, with great reluctance, everyone stopped what they were doing and rose to stand next to their piles of rubble. Mr Francis laughed as he observed the looks on their faces. 'Do not be disheartened,' he said. 'Today was mostly about team building. I think most of you have achieved this to a degree. There is still a long way for us to go, but many of the materials in front of you will need welding together. Welding is not typically a first day kind of thing.' He stroked his beard as he paced around the middle of the cave. 'We will come back to that. I do, however, have news that will come as a relief to some of you more than others,' he shot a twisted smile at Ellie's group, 'and that is that you can leave all of your bits on the floor, right where they are. We don't have to tidy anything away, because when we come back to it, we need to continue exactly from where we have left off. Any questions?' Ellie couldn't help but wonder if this was Mr Francis's general approach to life, and not just a happy class bylaw. Still, she approved of it, and she approved of him. When no one had any questions, Mr Francis said, 'Very well. Go forth, and I will see you next time.'

That night, as Ellie lay in bed and stared into the blankness of the unlit dormitory, her thoughts went back over Francis's class. What were they trying to build? The runners looked as though they provided a moving mechanism for a door or a hatch. She wished they had had more time to work at it. She felt sure that they were minutes away from making serious and notable advancements. She turned over in her bed and tried to concentrate on sleeping. She scrunched up her eyes as fresh desires to return to the basement and sort through the construction piled up inside her. Then she opened her eyes again with a sudden jolt. She had seen a face when she closed her eyes, and she couldn't understand it. She closed them again to make quite sure, and once again, the smiling, dark-eyebrowed, bright-eyed and charismatic face of Harvey stared back at her. She rolled over in her bed, thrusting her face deep into her pillow with embarrassment.

The following day, Ellie's desire to return for the second metal works class had not diminished. Jake and Dana had sat next to her at breakfast and noted her Speaking Aid with genuine interest. Ellie was, however, feeling somewhat distracted and a little jumpy. She answered their questions with minimal enthusiasm.

'Can you choose different accents for it?' Jake had asked.

'I suppose,' Ellie said.

'That would be great, wouldn't it?' said Dana. 'You could be Australian.'

'Sure.'

'What about Irish?' said Jake.

Ellie looked from one to the other. 'It wouldn't make any difference to me, would it?'

'But it would be funny,' said Dana.

'Yes, for everybody else but me.'

Dana placed a hand on Ellie's. 'I'm sorry,' she said. 'I didn't mean… that was stupid of me.'

'It's fine.'

Jake and Dana looked at each other in silent trepidation. 'How did your class go last night?' said Jake at last.

'Fine, thanks. Why?'

Jake smiled. 'Is that it?'

Again, the smiling face of Harvey popped suddenly up to the forefront of Ellie's mind. 'Well, what more do you want? It was good. Nothing else happened. Why the sudden interest?'

Jake and Dana looked at each other, nonplussed. Ellie felt the buzzer on her wrist signal that the bell was ringing for the first class of the day, and with some relief she stood up from the breakfast table and picked up her bag. 'What have we got first?'

Dana scrolled through her planner. 'Astronomy, it looks like.'

'Great,' said Ellie. 'Come on then.'

Jake stuffed the last half slice of toast into his mouth and followed, dropping crumbs as Ellie and Dana marched off in the direction of Mr Walters' classroom.

Mr Walters possessed the unfortunate knack of turning a perfectly interesting subject into an unyielding test of endurance. Ellie was well aware of this so resolved to make an extra effort to pay particular attention. For about the first ten minutes, Ellie concentrated hard on what Mr Walters was saying. She made notes to help her retain focus, but it was not only the things he was saying; it was his delivery. Each utterance appeared to be punctuated at random intervals by unnecessary pauses. His speech would also slacken and pick up pace in a confusing pattern that deviated from the regular structure of sentences. Ellie's eyelids grew heavy as she watched him talk.

At intervals, during his monologue, she thought of Harvey and her metal works group. She shook her head quickly to rid herself of these thoughts, but every time she refocussed on Mr Walters, something else would come along and take her attention away, within seconds. She could see Jake's star, through the window, though the sky was not yet completely dark. It was one of those wintery days that never really wakes up. The other stars were not yet visible in the gloom, but this one was. *That's curious.* She wondered again what it might be called. Mr Walters had always discoursed so drearily on the planets in the solar system that Ellie must not have retained it.

'Miss Webster.'

Curious especially, though, how the star was so big. Perhaps it was *so* big that it was visible from another solar system. *Perhaps it's not in our solar system at all,* she thought.

'Miss Webster.'

But even so, she considered over her bitten stylus. *It must have been mentioned. I wonder what it's called.*

'Miss Webster!'

Ellie thought this posed an interesting question for Mr Walters, and as she turned back to the class to venture it, she discovered that he was already staring back at her, his face the shade of a rich and dark plum.

'Miss Webster,' said Mr Walters, bubbling with indignation. 'Is there somewhere else you would rather be?'

Ellie felt that this had to be a trick question and so refrained from answering it honestly. 'No.'

'There's not something we're keeping you from?' persisted Mr Walters.

'No,' said Ellie.

'Enough!' said Mr Walters, clenching his fists in rage. He was an undersized and slightly blighted-looking man, and he pulled a handkerchief from his breast pocket, dabbing it carefully at patches of his forehead. 'Clearly there is,' he said. 'So I think the best thing would be for you to go there.'

Ellie regarded the man suspiciously. *This has to be a trick.*

'Just do one thing for me, Miss Webster. On your way to wherever it is, just stop in at Mrs Atkinson's office and explain to her what you're doing, would you? Because I'm not interested.'

Ellie began slowly to pack away her belongings. She felt as though Mr Walters was waiting for her to leave before continuing his lesson, and this caused her chest to constrict with humiliation. She felt the eyes of the other students upon her. She had never been dismissed from a class before. She had seen it happen to others, but it felt alien to her. She crept as unobtrusively as she could towards the door. She stole a final backwards glance as she pushed it open. Jake and Dana were watching her in open-mouthed incredulity. Walters said, 'Now then,' and she disappeared from view.

She walked through the deserted corridors, feeling despondent and shuffling her feet in an attempt to buy herself as much time as she could before having to explain anything to Mrs Atkinson. She wondered what she would say. *Sorry, I thought his class was so catastrophically boring that I was longing to be in a different one.* She looked guiltily over her shoulders as she passed more classrooms, quickening her pace as she passed the clear-panelled doors so as to reduce the likelihood of being seen.

She took the first flight of stairs, plodding slowly up each step, praying for some kind of intervention to occur. When she reached the top, still nothing had, and it was with great reluctance that she turned down the corridor that would ultimately lead her to Mrs Atkinson's office.

She stopped outside the door, swallowed a lump in her throat and stood with her hand outstretched towards the door. She stalled for a moment and then knocked.

Mrs Atkinson was on her way back from the cafeteria when Ellie was knocking at her office door. She had been waiting for the nozzle on the coffee machine to drip its final drops of whipped milk into her Styrofoam cup. She looked tired and she stirred three sachets of sugar into the cup before she turned, head bowed, back towards the exit. So absorbed was she in the meticulous stirring of her drink that she did not see a tall, dark figure approaching from the other direction.

'Do you like a little coffee with your sugar, or what?'

She looked up with a start and placed a hand to her chest. 'Oh, Stanley. You frightened me.'

'Sorry,' said Mr Harrison. 'Which way are you going?'

'Back to my office.'

'Mind if I walk with you?'

'Not at all.'

'I was hoping to find you. I've been meaning to ask how morale is doing among the troops.'

Mrs Atkinson rolled her eyes. 'Don't ask.'

'That good, huh?'

'Well, let's see,' she said. 'Mr Everton wants a meeting with Le Dich. More precisely, he wants *me* to have a meeting with Le Dich. He and Walters would have me grovel to save that programme, which, frankly, I am not above doing. Eileen wants me to try the fundraising idea, which is all well and good, but who do we target with that?'

'What do *you* want to do, Yvette?' said Mr Harrison. 'What do *you* think is best?'

'I couldn't tell you what is best,' said Mrs Atkinson. 'I do know that I don't relish the idea of meeting with Le Dich.'

'That could be done via holographic link,' said Mr Harrison. 'It's not like you would have to meet in person.'

'Even by holographic link, I wouldn't relish it,' she said, sipping her coffee. 'The man's quite deranged, Stanley.'

Mr Harrison pursed his lips. 'Quite,' he said, feeling chastened.

They were rounding the corner to her office.

'I mean, I can't see where the programme has failed, can you?'

Mr Harrison nibbled his bottom lip and shook his head.

'They put a system in place, ask us to deliver. We deliver and they say, "Sorry, that's enough, no more flight-to-freedom programme."'

She looked at Mr Harrison for his reaction, but Mr Harrison had stopped walking. He was staring fixedly ahead. She followed his eye until it rested upon a small girl, whose knee-length socks had gathered loosely about her ankles. The girl was standing outside her office door, clasping the straps of a backpack and staring back at them defiantly.

'Ellie Webster,' breathed Mrs Atkinson.

SEVEN

ELLIE STARED AT the two teachers, slowly shifting her body weight from one leg to the other, her socks bunching around her ankles. It would be impossible to pretend that she had not seen them talking. Harder still was to gauge just how they were going to react to her. Ellie liked Mrs Atkinson, but Mr Harrison was slightly more of an unknown. She had only had very limited dealings with him in the past and could not be sure what to expect of him. In the end, it was Mr Harrison who spoke first.

'Ellie,' he said with an irritation he struggled hopelessly to conceal. 'What are you doing here? Why aren't you in your class?' Ellie could see the colour rising to his face. 'There are very severe consequences for this sort of thing,' he went on. 'I mean, how—'

'Stanley,' said Mrs Atkinson calmly, 'if Ellie were the type to skip class, which I don't believe she is, do you think it likely that she would hide out next to my office? I should think Ellie has something to talk to me about. Is that right, Ellie?' Ellie nodded thoughtfully. 'There you are; you see? I dare say it is a matter best kept between Ellie and myself.' Her face became stony and she dropped her voice. 'Leave us, Stanley. I will deal with it.'

Mr Harrison was reluctant to leave the scene, but he knew better than to try and overrule her. 'Very well,' he said at last. He backed away slowly and Mrs Atkinson waited patiently until he was completely out of sight before she turned her attention back to Ellie. 'OK,' she said with a deep sigh, 'you'd better come in and have a seat.'

Ellie sat down in front of Mrs Atkinson's desk and watched with wide, innocent eyes as the teacher removed her robe and hung it on the back of her chair. Underneath she wore a grey pinstriped suit. She looked very smart, the kind of smart that Ellie felt she was never likely to achieve herself. Mrs Atkinson sat down opposite Ellie and busied herself with stirring her coffee and arranging the picture frames on her desk. Ellie waited, wondering if she was expected to speak first. After several minutes had passed and neither of them had said a word, Ellie began to find the total lack of conversation oppressive. She decided to deal the opening hand. 'Mrs Atkinson, I'm sorry I'm out of class. Mr Walters said—'

'I'm glad to see you are making use of your Speaking Aid,' said Mrs Atkinson without looking up. She crossed her legs, shuffled in her seat and blew into her coffee cup.

'Yes.' Ellie hesitated. 'I hope it's working. I can't hear it, but—'

Mrs Atkinson looked up and met Ellie's eye. 'It's working,' she said.

Ellie gave a stifled laugh. 'Good. Look, Mrs Atkinson, I—'

'How much did you see, Ellie?'

'What? I... how much did I—'

'How much did you see me say, or hear me say; you know what I mean. I was talking with Mr Harrison when we bumped into you. How much of our conversation did you understand?'

Ellie's face resigned itself to total sincerity. 'Something about how the programme has failed,' she said. 'No more flights-to-freedom—'

'Good,' said Mrs Atkinson. 'That's what I thought.' She flicked her hair away from her face and sipped her drink. 'What did you conclude from this?'

'I didn't conclude anything,' said Ellie.

'Oh, come on,' snapped Mrs Atkinson. 'I know you're smarter than that.' She leaned forward in her seat and placed her cup on the desk. She smiled a well-practised smile and exhaled through her nostrils. 'Talk to me, Ellie.'

Ellie sighed. 'The Legion is going to abort the flight-to-freedom programme. My guess is that it's going to be soon.'

Mrs Atkinson watched her closely. 'You're right,' she said at last. 'The programme is to be abolished. We only found out for sure yesterday. This year's Level Twelves are going to be the last.' Ellie did not know what to say, and for the next few moments she sat and blinked in silence.

'We do not yet know what shape the system will take after this year,' Mrs Atkinson continued. 'Having no answer to this, I have held off making an announcement to the school. Unfortunately, you have witnessed this conversation, and that cannot be undone. I do hope, however, that you will practise discretion and not mention this to all of your friends before I have had a chance to gain a greater understanding of what is going to happen next.'

Ellie shook her head automatically.

'I will, of course, understand if you feel the need to talk to somebody,' went on Mrs Atkinson. 'My door is open to you, Ellie. If ever you feel troubled by what you have learned today and feel in need of some answers, come and find me. I will be here for you, and when we have a fuller understanding of the implications of this development, the rest of the school will be told; you have my word.'

Ellie nodded. 'OK,' she said through her Speaking Aid.

Mrs Atkinson sat back in her chair and turned her attention towards the window. Ellie wasn't sure whether or not to take this as a dismissal, and she reached down to clasp the handles of her bag, but just then Mrs Atkinson spoke again. 'Now, Ellie, don't think for a moment that I've forgotten there must have been another reason for your being outside my office.' Ellie let the straps of her bag slip between her fingers and land back on the office floor. Mrs Atkinson folded her arms. 'What's happened?'

Mrs Atkinson escorted Ellie back to her Astronomy class, in time to catch the final five minutes. Mr Walters at first received her knock at the door with further bluster and outrage, but then he spotted Mrs Atkinson standing behind the girl, with a hand on her shoulder.

'Mr Walters,' said Mrs Atkinson serenely. 'Thank you for sending Miss Webster to see me. How could you have known that she had quite forgotten to pass on to me an important message regarding her application for enrolment in the metal works programme? The deadline is, of course, noon today, and she should have missed it were it not for you.'

Mr Walters spluttered, 'Bu… bu… but I—'

'You have done a noble thing,' said Mrs Atkinson, flashing him her warmest smile. She turned on her heel, then looked back as though another thought had just crossed her mind. 'Incidentally,' she said, 'I may require Miss Webster's assistance over the next couple of weeks. She is helping me with something that I will be announcing later on in the year. Should Miss Webster be required to leave your classroom again, I know you will extend to her your absolute patience and understanding, won't you?' Mr Walters stammered again, but Mrs Atkinson's face was an enigma. 'Thank you,' she said, as his stammering recoiled under her gaze.

Jake and Dana looked at Ellie in amazement. 'Are you going to tell us what that was all about?' Jake whispered as she returned to her seat, but Ellie placed a finger to her lips and winked at him.

When the bell rang for a class break a few minutes later, Ellie made her way with Jake and Dana to the common room. She used her school credit card to buy herself a coffee. Jake and Dana watched bewildered as she sat cross-legged on a chair and stirred her drink methodically with a wooden spoon, imagining herself to be the picture of sophistication. 'Since when did you start drinking coffee?' Jake scoffed. Ellie made no comment. Her eyes wore a faraway look, as her mind replayed the conversation with Mrs Atkinson.

'What happened?' asked Dana. Ellie considered. She would have to talk to Jake and Dana eventually; but she had promised Mrs Atkinson she wouldn't. What if Atkinson took too long to make her announcement? Surely Jake and Dana deserved to know as much as she did, but what *did* she know? She cradled her head in her hands as the different corners of her conscience fought. All she knew was that there was a problem; she did not yet know how it would be resolved, so by telling them what she knew now, she would only be spreading fear. She wrestled with the morality of the dilemma for a few more minutes, and when she looked back up, her friends had disappeared. Ellie leaped to her feet and made a cursory inspection of the common room and outside corridor, but they were nowhere to be seen.

Ellie didn't see either of them before or after her afternoon history class, so after the school day was over she had another look for them. This again turned out to be fruitless and they still had not turned up by the time Ellie was making her way down to dinner. She sat alone, picking at the burnt bits of cheese on the top of her lasagne in solitary despondency. She was, in fact, fairly relieved when it came time to go to bed. At least, she supposed, she would see Dana then; but it wasn't to be. As Ellie lay in her bunk, staring up at the underside of Dana's mattress, fear, annoyance and curiosity kept her mind going round and round in a loop of unanswerable questions.

At some point during the fractious night, Ellie woke with a start. She had not been aware that she had been asleep, but she must have been, for the sensation of the bed lurching roused her from it. She just had time to catch a glimpse of Dana's feet disappearing over the top of the bunk. Ellie couldn't say what time it was, but it was still dark outside. She thought about checking the time, but even as the thought crossed her mind, she fell back into another uneasy snooze.

The following morning, Ellie jumped out of bed and inspected Dana's bunk with interest, but Dana was already gone. For that matter, everyone was gone. She looked around the floor at their scattered belongings, her eyes resting on a pair of trainers that looked as though they had been kicked off and discarded in haste. Ellie picked one up and inspected it more closely. The sole was caked in mud, and she suddenly realised where they must have been. Hurt and indignation rising within her, she threw a robe over her shoulders and hastened down to the main hall.

Jake and Dana were sitting with the other Level Twelves and chatting together over a hearty-looking breakfast of pancakes and maple syrup. She strode over to their table and sat down, hugging her robe around her middle and swinging her feet under the table.

'Hi, Ellie,' said Dana with surprise. 'Why aren't you dressed?'

'Did you two go to the treehouse last night?' asked Ellie with a frown.

'Yes,' said Jake.

'Why didn't you invite me?'

'Because you didn't seem to want to talk to us,' said Jake. 'You seemed too busy, planning your next get-out-of-astronomy-class-free mission.'

'That's not true,' Ellie said.

'Isn't it?'

'No. I haven't been planning anything, but something happened yesterday when I went to Atkinson's office and I didn't know how to tell you.'

'Just tell us,' said Jake with a shrug.

Ellie looked furtively around, but her state of undress was attracting looks from all corners of the hall. 'I can't tell you *now*,' she said.

'Well, what about tonight?' Dana asked.

'Fine. Oh… except I have metal works tonight.'

'Whatever,' said Jake, rising from his seat and slinging his bag over his shoulders. 'You'd better get dressed, you'll be late for class. That is, if you still go to classes.'

Ellie looked at Dana, who was smiling at her sadly. 'You can talk to us, you know? When you're ready.' Ellie gathered to speak, but Dana continued, 'You really ought to get dressed, Ellie. People are looking.' Ellie frowned and hunched her shoulders as Dana scurried off after Jake. She stared furiously around at the other students, who hastily lowered their gazes.

Ellie spent a miserable morning, attending classes where Jake and Dana had little to do with her. During the afternoon, they had been split into pairs for one of Mr Adlington's geography lessons. Ellie cradled her head in her hands as Jake and Dana immediately separated themselves from her without a word. She imagined that she would be the only person in the class without a partner, and that Mr Adlington would either use himself to make up a consolation pair or simply assign her to an existing pair to make up one slightly awkward group of three. She buried her face in her desk while she considered which was the lesser of the two evils.

It was then that she felt a tap on her shoulder. Slowly, she raised her head and turned to see which hand fate had delivered. Harvey stood next to her desk with a ruler in his hand and a stylus tucked neatly behind his ear. 'Hi, Ellie,' he said, revealing a set of perfect teeth. 'Want to partner up?'

'What?' came the blurted response from the Speaking Aid.

'Well, I thought we worked pretty well together the other night,' said Harvey. 'Care to give it another try?' Ellie grinned and hastily pulled out a chair for him to sit down. 'Thanks,' said Harvey. 'Are you going on the Peak District trip?'

Ellie nodded enthusiastically. 'Yes.'

'Me too. I suppose we'll see all this stuff for real, huh? It's got to be better than learning from books and theory. I prefer interactive learning. Hence why I signed up for metal works.'

Ellie nodded again. 'Yes, exactly.'

Harvey and Ellie chatted away as they worked at their landmass studies. It cannot be said, however, that their hearts were entirely in it. Both were looking forward to the second metal works class, which was to take place that evening after school; and when the final bell rang, they walked together to the common room, where they snacked on biscuits and chatted more about their Level Twelves. Harvey apparently had great expectations for the Level Twelves and life aboard the safe station. He told Ellie that he longed to be a pilot. He wanted to be the one flying the shuttles on the flight-to-freedom programme.

'They're always looking for pilots,' he had said. 'It's a very successful programme.' Ellie turned pink when she inhaled some of her coffee the wrong way and Harvey had to pat her on the back until the coughing had subsided. 'Are you alright?'

'I'm fine,' said Ellie, her eyes brimming. 'We'd better go, or we're going to miss it.'

They walked together to the main hall, where they saw a bunch of boys from the class huddled around the lift doors. They all stepped into the lift together and Ellie braced herself, but the doors closed softly, and the lift glided down to the basement easily and steadily. Everybody looked relieved.

'Welcome, welcome,' called out Mr Francis as they all stepped from the lift into the basement cave. 'Please go and stand next to your projects in your groups. We will start just as soon as everybody has arrived.'

As the students made their way over to the untouched piles of rubble from two days previously, the lift was called back to the surface. It returned, depositing several more students at the cave's entrance – including Doug and Nick, who joined Ellie and Harvey in standing thoughtfully over their discarded pile. The lift performed two more journeys before everybody stood in the hall, looking at Mr Francis with upturned, expectant faces.

'Good,' he said as he scanned the group. 'Everybody is here. Today you are going to map out your project in stages. You will get as far as you can, following the booklet and using the hand tools provided. At some point, you will find that you cannot progress without the larger tools. You may find that you need a section welded, soldered or drilled. At this point and not before you will come and see me. I will go through the process with you and we will learn a little more about how to handle these tools. Do not come and see me until you have to. I want you to get absolutely as far as you can without me.'

Ellie and Harvey looked at each other excitedly, then they all fell upon their projects with renewed vigour. Nick and Doug were working more or less as their own unit, and Ellie and Harvey did the same. The divide slowed their progress somewhat, and all four of them felt frustrated when Mr Francis called everybody's attention to the fact that one of the other groups had been the first to reach a legitimate point at which they could step up to using the big tools.

Mr Francis stopped everybody and asked that they pay attention as he demonstrated the handling of a blowtorch. Everybody moved into a semi-circle, placed protective lenses over their eyes and watched eagerly as he removed his jacket and shut the visor down over his face. He gave a few further superficial instructions through the visor (which Harvey relayed to Ellie) about how best to hold the blowtorch. He then proceeded to demonstrate upon the metal structure of the other group's build.

As Mr Francis worked away, the flame meeting with the metal assembly and illuminating the sea of watching faces with a rich and golden glow, something distracted Ellie. Where Mr Francis had removed his jacket to reveal a grey and oil-stained T-shirt, his sleeve had rolled back over his bicep as he gripped and aimed the blowtorch. There, etched into his right arm in black ink, was the partially revealed tattoo of an emblem depicting three interlocking 'L's. Everybody else was watching what he was doing with the blowtorch. She nudged Harvey in the ribs.

'Oi,' he said, 'what's up?'

Ellie nodded towards Mr Francis's upper arm. 'What is that?'

Harvey squinted through the flickering light. 'It looks like a Legion tattoo,' he considered.

'Does that mean Mr Francis is Legion?'

'It might,' said Harvey with a puzzled frown. 'But what…'

'What's he doing here?' Ellie finished.

EIGHT

As September trickled into October, the chill bit slightly harder and the days ran a little shorter. Dormitory checks were being administered more stringently, since the risk of catching viruses had increased with the bad weather.

Although the behaviour of the students was being monitored more closely, it had been some time since Ellie had even felt tempted to try and escape to her treehouse. The weather was reflecting the overall mood of the school. Jake was still rather moodily keeping out of Ellie's way, but she was preoccupied with fresh concerns, anyhow – namely, the story of Mr Francis.

The metal works class had shrunk a little in the wake of the creeping cold. With more and more afflicted students, progress on the mystery constructions had slowed right down. Ellie's team had lost Nick for the last two sessions and this had brought about a change in the group dynamic. Doug now operated more cohesively with her and Harvey, but Ellie considered the relationship purely a working one, and as such, he was not to be included in speculative conversations about Mr Francis and his Legion association. She and Harvey reserved these discussions for in between classes and after school.

'Maybe he just supports the Legion,' suggested Harvey as they made their way back up to the ground floor, following a strenuous evening in which they had had to pot rivet a door frame to a made-to-measure panel.

Ellie bit her lip and said, 'Maybe,' but she looked doubtful.

'Well,' said Harvey, 'if he was actually part of the Legion, he would be there, wouldn't he? No one comes back, do they?' Ellie considered this in silence as they vaulted the last few steps to the common room. They paused at the top as Ellie noticed Jake leaving the room and making a beeline for his dormitory floor. Her gaze followed him until he was nearly out of sight, then she suddenly realised that Harvey was still talking to her.

'What's up?' she caught him saying. 'You didn't see anything I just said, did you?'

'Sorry.'

Harvey glanced over his shoulder in time to see Jake's back just before it had disappeared from view. 'Why don't you go and talk to him?'

'I will,' said Ellie, folding her arms. 'Later.'

When Ellie entered the dining hall an hour later, she made her way over to Dana and Jake, who sat in furtive conversation. They both fell silent as she settled into a seat next to them and looked at her expectantly.

'Hello,' came the mechanical emanation from the Speaking Aid.

Jake mumbled something and Dana said, 'Hi, Ellie.'

'What are you talking about?'

'Laurie Humphries,' said Jake.

'What?'

'Dana's sister. Remember?'

'Oh, right,' said Ellie. 'Have you found anything?'

'Not yet,' said Dana. She lowered her voice to a whisper and leaned closer. 'We've been sneaking out to the forest most nights lately.'

Ellie's heart burned a little at this revelation, but she kept her face placid.

'Laurie used to have a GPS tracker set up on her work pad,' said Dana. 'I had one too. Our parents used it to keep an eye on us.'

'Do you still have it?'

'I do,' said Dana, 'but there's a problem.'

'What?'

'Our devices were never linked. Even if she were alive and here on Earth, and even if she still had the same work pad, we can't easily trace her without a linked device.'

'Even if we could,' said Jake, 'we'd only get the location of the work pad, not necessarily her location.'

'It would be a start,' said Ellie. 'Can't you just send a request from your work pad to link up with Laurie Humphries?'

'We tried the other night,' said Dana, 'but there's a million Laurie Humphries out there, and with no picture reference, it's pretty much impossible.'

'Well, we'll just have to work our way through the list,' said Ellie.

'I know,' said Dana. 'It could take weeks, and there's no guarantee of success.'

Ellie squeezed her arm. 'I will help you,' she said.

Dana smiled, then fixed Ellie with her penetrating stare. 'What's been going on with you, anyway?'

Ellie buckled under the stare and shifted her glance between Dana and Jake and the surrounding area, until it rested guiltily on her own toes. 'I'm sorry,' she said. 'I'm sorry I haven't told you about what happened at Atkinson's office.'

Jake shrugged, but Dana leaned forward in her seat. 'You'll tell us now, won't you, Ellie?' She looked at Jake for encouragement. 'What did happen?'

Ellie looked from one to the other, but before she could articulate a response, Jake and Dana shot a simultaneous and startled glance over their shoulders towards the entrance of the main hall. Ellie looked from them to the doorway in surprise. The other students were also staring at exactly the same spot. She hesitated. The teachers were darting towards the door.

'What is it?'

Some students stood up from their tables. Others craned their necks to see what had happened. Mrs Atkinson was near the door, addressing her colleagues, but she was too far away for Ellie to make out the words. She clasped Jake's hand and he jolted, looking back at her, clearly distracted.

'What's going on?' she said.

Jake looked back towards the entrance door that Mrs Atkinson had just left through. Mr Everton, Mr Walters and Mr Adlington stood in the doorway, barring the curious crowd that was gathering there. 'I don't know,' he said. 'There was like some kind of crash outside. Atkinson told us all to stay here.'

Ellie stood up and climbed onto the seat of her pew. The crowd of students was thickening and she had to stand on the tips of her toes to see over all of the heads. When Mrs Atkinson returned, her face was pale, but she straightened herself importantly.

'She's going to say something.'

Mrs Atkinson waited for the commotion to subside. She cleared her throat and addressed the congregation. 'There has been an accident in the main hall.' A clamour of excited voices rose from portions of the audience, and Ellie waited impatiently as Mrs Atkinson waited again for it to die down. 'The ceiling of the main hall appears to have been struck and a portion has given way.' There was further outcry from the students, and Mrs Atkinson put up her hands for quiet.

'You will return to your dormitories in your Level Groups,' she called out. 'You will be escorted by your Level Leaders and you will pass through the main hall extremely carefully. Do not stray from your group. Return to your rooms quickly and carefully.' She threw a worried glance back towards the door, then continued. 'Tomorrow, those of you who are going to the Peak District will assemble outside at 9am. A breakfast will be provided for you on the Aquabus. Those travelling home for the holidays and those staying here will wait in their dormitories until called upon for breakfast.' More questions followed in a cacophony of mass hysteria and confusion, but Mrs Atkinson waved them firmly away. 'Everyone return to your seats, please. Everyone except Level Twelve – Level Twelve will leave first.'

Ellie's peer group was packed into a tight huddle and escorted from the room amidst plenty of finger-pointing and directional commands from the teachers. As they shuffled through to the main hall there was a collective gasp as everyone caught sight of the devastation for the first time. They looked from the pile of rubble that had fallen through and cracked the stone floor, to the gaping hole way overhead. A gentle flurry of something between snow and rain was cascading down through the crevice. Ellie shivered. The building was incredibly old, and the stone bricks that lay in an inert mass on the floor varied in shades of pink, brown and beige.

As they shunted onwards, everyone was looking upwards at the hole in the ceiling, but something on the ground had attracted Ellie's attention. Amongst the heap of stone on the floor was something smaller than a brick and rounder in shape. It was jet-black and glistened under the light. She shot discreet glances at the other students, but nobody else seemed to have even seen it. *What is that?*

The procession was slow-moving as they skirted the debris and were led to the stairway. Ellie had become slightly separated from Jake and Dana as the group shifted and started mounting the steps. He looked back at her as they climbed up in their knotted cluster. She tried to sign to him, 'I'll talk to you tomorrow,' but she could not be sure he had understood; there were too many heads and bodies moving and jostling between them.

Back in their dorm, Dana nudged Ellie. 'What were you going to tell us before?'

'I'll tell you both tomorrow,' said Ellie, 'when we are on the Aquabus.' Dana looked disappointed but nodded and climbed up to her bunk.

It was not easy for anyone to drift off that night. There was an icy chill in the air brought on by the new hole in the roof, and though Ellie didn't know it, there was the added commotion of Mr Francis walking about on the roof, tacking vinyl screens over the hole with lock tight pins and fast-hardening gel.

Ellie's thoughts danced between curiosity over what the strange oval object had been in the rubble and disquiet over the saddened look in Dana's eyes when she had chosen again not to confide in her.

She lay still on her back, feeling the rock of the bed every time Dana fidgeted or rolled over above. She couldn't sleep either. She looked out of the window. Jake's star seemed to be burning brighter than ever and Ellie smiled at the memory of sitting with him in the treehouse. Then a shadow passed over her face and she scowled in thought. She looked carefully about her, then climbed stealthily out of bed. Rotating on the spot, she looked all around the room, catching her breath when she came face to face with Dana, who was leaning over the side of the top bunk. 'What are you doing?'

'Come on,' said Ellie. 'I'll show you.'

Dana wavered, but Ellie turned and stepped lightly over to the dormitory door. Eyes wide with fear, Dana slipped silently down the ladder of her bunk and scurried over to the door that Ellie held open for her. They crept quietly out along the hallway. Ellie was making her way straight to the main stairway, and Dana followed in soft, dance-like steps.

As she reached the top of the stairs, Ellie peered over the rail and down to the heap of bricks. She halted and stepped back from the bannister.

Dana froze mid step. 'What is it?' she whispered.

'Mr Francis is down there.'

They both looked up to the patched hole in the roof. 'We shouldn't be out here, Ellie.'

Ellie ignored this advice and crouched down below the bannister, clasping the ornate metal uprights with her hands and poking her head out as far as she could. She could just see Mr Francis. He was squatting down in front of the rubble. As though hypnotised, Dana moved over to sit beside her. She also pressed her face as far as she could through the rails to see what Ellie was looking at.

An old-fashioned shovel lay on the ground next to Mr Francis. He had evidently started to clear away the mess and something had stopped him in his tracks. He was moving bricks carefully aside with his hands now, and slowly he extracted the black, shiny, oval brick that Ellie had been puzzling over.

'You see that?'

'Yes,' said Dana, craning her neck.

'What is it?'

'It looks like the *Pablucto Silvantes*,' said Dana. 'Only bigger.'

'What?'

'You know, the pebble projectors we used in Adlington's class.'

Ellie looked back over the precipice. Mr Francis was turning the object over in his hands. He looked as though he were not entirely sure what to do with it. Then he threw a quick glance over his shoulders, rose from the pile of bricks and made his way across the main hall and out of sight.

'Come on,' said Ellie, leaping to her feet and bouncing down the stairs.

'Wait,' hissed Dana; but it was too late. Ellie was already halfway down to the next floor. Dana scrunched her toes anxiously and followed on.

Ellie reached the bottom step in time to see Mr Francis enter a small corridor, jutting off ahead and to their right. When Dana had caught up, she was panting nervously; but before she could stop to catch her breath, Ellie was off again, beckoning for Dana to follow.

Dana no longer made any attempt at protest. She swallowed, took a deep breath and kept pace with Ellie as they sped over the cold stone floor in bare-footed unison. They skidded round the corner to the corridor Mr Francis had taken. Towards the far end, they saw him gently prise open a classroom door and disappear within.

They sprinted down towards the room, slowing on the final approach. With their faces pressed up to the small window in the door, they watched as Mr Francis settled himself into a chair at one of the students' tables. Turning the pebble round in his hands, he inspected the device for an 'On' switch. When the projection finally came on, it was directed towards the floor and Mr Francis jumped in surprise. Carefully, he arranged the light so that it pointed at the back wall behind the teacher's desk.

A large face stared down at him. Ellie and Dana looked to one another for an answer, but each was as dumfounded as the other. Neither one of them recognised the face. It had startlingly bright blue eyes, dark and well-groomed hair, and thin red lips. It would have been an attractive face, were it not for the icy, conceited expression that carried through to Ellie and Dana a feeling of deep foreboding.

When it spoke, it said, 'I will keep this brief,' in a voice that could have cut glass. Dana shivered and Mr Francis flinched, but Ellie fixated closely on the movement of the lips. 'Just in case this has fallen into the wrong hands, I will simply say that my end is taken care of. There should now be a hole in the roof of the school. This is the excuse you need. Do not go to the Peak District tomorrow, but stay behind and repair the damage. Do it quickly, mind you. You need to get into Atkinson's office and find every Level Twelve student file. We need that data. It goes without saying that we need to know more about who we've got coming through this year. Get me those files.'

Dana gave a sudden jump and clapped Ellie on the shoulder with the back of her hand. Ellie tore her eyes away from the face in time to see Dana mouth, 'Run!'

Ellie understood that there must be an imminent threat. Dana must have heard someone else approaching. She didn't stop to question it. She followed Dana across the corridor to the classroom on the opposite side. They closed the door behind them and watched nervously through the pane to see who it was.

Mr Harrison appeared in the hallway. He stopped with his back to them and pushed open the door to the room in which Mr Francis sat. As the door swung shut behind him, it caught on the latch, and through the crack Ellie and Dana could see the light of the projection still flickering. 'Come on,' said Ellie, 'we need to see what they're saying.' Dana gulped but followed Ellie back out into the darkened hallway. Cautiously, they repositioned themselves in front of the door and peered once more through the windowpane.

Mr Harrison stood directly on the other side, still with his back to them. His position was such that he had inadvertently obscured the view they had had of Mr Francis and the projection. Ellie could not make out a single word of the conversation and she looked at Dana desperately. 'Can you hear anything?'

'It's hard,' said Dana. 'The message is playing again, and they're arguing over it.' She pressed her ear to the crack in the door. 'They're arguing about which one of them should stay behind tomorrow.'

Ellie looked back to see if she could see anything of their faces. The message seemed to be finishing, and the face was grinning a cold and sinister smile. There did seem to be some arm-waving going on between the two men. Ellie wondered if they were going to hit each other. It looked as though there was a brief struggle over the pebble, and as Ellie's heart pounded with excitement and nerves, she instinctively put a hand to the door. She withdrew it sharply, but the damage had already been done. The door swung an inch forward before falling back into the frame with the satisfying click of the perfect fit.

Ellie could only imagine how loud a click it had been, but as she looked to her left, Dana was already fleeing the corridor.

Mr Francis and Mr Harrison stopped arguing for a moment. Both men looked towards the door.

'Who's there?' called out Mr Harrison.

'No one,' said Mr Francis. 'The door is weighted. You must have left it open.'

Mr Harrison ignored him and, still staring at the door, moved over to inspect. He swung it back violently. His blood was up, and he threw frantic glances up and across the corridor that Ellie and Dana had just escaped from, but Ellie and Dana *had* escaped and Mr Francis was quite right: there was no one there at all.

NINE

'HE WAS SAYING he wanted him to stay behind and not go on the trip,' Dana explained excitedly.

'Wait, who said that?' said Jake.

'Le Dich,' said Ellie. Jake and Dana both looked at her askance, but she only shrugged at them. 'It had to be him.'

The three of them had assembled with the rest of the students in the main hall, where they all waited for the Aquabus that would take them to the Peak District.

'He wanted *who* to stay behind?' Jake asked.

'Mr Francis,' exclaimed Dana.

'Not necessarily,' said Ellie.

'What do you mean?' said Jake.

'Francis is the one that found the message,' explained Ellie. 'It doesn't necessarily mean that it was meant for him. At the beginning Le Dich says he'll keep the message brief "in case it has fallen into the wrong hands".'

'Well,' said Dana, folding her arms. 'I think it had to be for him. He was the one fixing the roof in the night. He knew exactly where to find the message...'

'…and he has a Legion tattoo on his arm,' came a new voice. Jake and Dana turned on the spot and Ellie craned her neck to see what they were looking at. Harvey stood on the edge of the circle with a bag slung loosely over his shoulder. He smiled his best and most charming smile.

'He has a what?' said Jake.

'A Legion tattoo on his right arm,' said Harvey.

'Does he?' said Jake, stroking his chin. 'That's weird.'

Ellie stamped her foot. 'It doesn't mean he's the spy,' she said.

'Go on, Ellie, *then* what happened?' prompted Jake.

'Then Harrison turned up, and they started arguing.'

'That's when we nearly got caught,' said Dana. 'It looked like they were having an argument about which one would stay behind.'

'No one can be above suspicion,' said Jake wisely. 'I know you like Francis, Ellie, but you have to admit that the evidence is pretty well stacked against him at the moment. That said, we shouldn't rule it out that Francis just got to the message first by chance. It could be for anyone.'

This measured assessment mollified the group sufficiently that Ellie began to turn her attention towards breakfast. 'I'm hungry,' she said.

'Atkinson said we'd have breakfast on the Aquabus,' said Harvey.

'Well, where is she, then?' said Jake. 'Where's the bus? I could eat.'

Just then, Ellie caught sight of the head as she stepped out from an office at the back of the main hall. She watched as Mr Francis intercepted her.

'There she is,' said Ellie, pointing. They all looked over.

'He's saying something to her,' said Harvey. 'What do you suppose he's saying?'

'We don't have to suppose,' said Jake. He looked at Ellie, who gave him a knowing nod. He then crouched down and allowed her to climb onto his back. With a little more difficulty than he would have liked to admit, he stood up again. Ellie now had a clearer view over the sea of heads, and she squinted hard as she concentrated on the movement of their lips.

'He's asking her if he should stay to fix the roof,' said Ellie.

'Just as he was instructed to do by Le Dich,' clarified Dana.

'Hang on,' said Ellie. 'Look.' They all craned their necks to see. 'Harrison's there too, and Adlington.'

Jake tugged her foot until she looked down at him. 'What are *they* saying?'

'They're saying the same thing,' said Ellie. 'That it should be them that stay behind and fix the roof.'

'What about Atkinson?' Harvey asked.

'She's not having it. She's saying she'll hire a professional, and they can all go on the trip. They all look pretty worried. Now Ulsworthy's getting involved. She's…' Ellie ducked her head and slid down Jake's back, landing on the floor with a soft thud. She looked up at them all, smiling ruefully. 'Atkinson saw me looking at her.'

Mrs Atkinson did look stressed when she approached the gathering. She spoke with a kind, but firm, delivery. 'I thought I asked you all to wait outside.'

'It's raining,' someone said.

'Is it?' She glanced at her watch. 'Never mind, the bus will be here now.' She flung open the entrance gate and scuttled across the tarmac to the waiting bus. After exchanging a few short words with the driver, the doors slid back and she motioned for the students to start boarding.

They all trooped out and she checked their names off on her work pad as they went. Ellie, Jake, Dana and Harvey got into line and boarded the bus in single file. Ellie was the last of the four, and as she stepped up, Mrs Atkinson placed a hand on her shoulder. 'Is everything alright, Ellie?'

'Yes, thanks.'

'Remember, you have any concerns, you talk to *me*.'

'I will.'

She held Ellie's gaze for another moment, then said, 'Go on then. Enjoy the trip.' Ellie nodded and climbed the steps up into the Aquabus, which was far bigger than the regular school busses. The seats were laid out in fours and positioned around fixed tables. Each compartment was separated by transparent plexiglass divides, and the only natural light came in through a small circular window, which was triple-glazed and extremely thick.

Jake was waving to her from a compartment at the back. 'Come on,' he said. 'We're in here.' Ellie grinned as she bundled over to them. She threw her bag into an overhead locker and Jake slid the compartment door shut behind her. As they settled into their seats, what looked like a light fitting overhead became illuminated and from it a holographic projection of a stewardess appeared and addressed them on the health and safety features provided on board. Through the plexiglass screens they could see half a dozen or so other stewardesses appear as the other compartments filled up and cubicle doors were closed.

Their stewardess smiled benignly and flitted between languages as Harvey played with the settings on the control panel. Eventually he found and selected *sign language*, whereupon the stewardess seamlessly and obediently began to speak and sign the instructions simultaneously. Ellie gave him a resigned smile. 'Thank you,' she said.

When the image of the stewardess had wished them a pleasant onward journey and flickered back out of sight, Jake cleared his throat and addressed the others. 'We have a lot to discuss,' he said. 'Fortunately we have a long ride ahead of us, so we should be able to cover everything.' He looked at Harvey, who was still inspecting the control panel. 'Harvey, some of what we are about to say might not make much sense to you at first. We don't know you as well as Ellie does, but we will explain.' As an afterthought, he added, 'And we'd also like to hear about the metal works class at some point.'

'No problem,' Harvey agreed.

Jake turned to the others. 'We need to discuss Dana's sister, Laurie. We need to discuss the message from Le Dich and we need to discuss what happened in Ellie's meeting with Atkinson last month.' Everyone nodded. 'Dana?'

Dana nodded again and explained for Harvey's benefit: 'My sister has been missing for the last three years. She may very well be dead, but there is also a chance she is on the safe station. We are trying to find her on Earth using GPS, but the process is long and tedious.'

'We will help you with that,' put in Ellie.

'What would be helpful,' said Jake, 'would be if we came up with some ideas about how to narrow the search. Literally any ideas from you guys would be helpful at this point. Me and Dana have knackered our brains out on this, and some fresh thinking could really help to get us going again.'

'Got it,' said Harvey.

'As far as the Le Dich message goes, who knows,' said Jake. 'You two saw it. Can you tell us any more, Ellie?'

'We saw part of it,' Ellie amended. 'We saw the beginning.' She puffed her cheeks. 'He was speaking directly to someone in our school. Probably a teacher. Whoever it is must be a spy, because in the message, he asks for this person to leak confidential files to him. He has created a diversion with the hole in the roof. He then instructs the spy to stay behind from the Peak District trip so as to fix the hole and leak the material.'

'Mr Francis looks the most likely to be the spy at this point,' said Dana.

'You two might have more to say on that,' said Jake to Ellie and Harvey. 'You know him better than we do, and of course there is the tattoo, which you mentioned.'

'So,' said Harvey, weighing up the possible scenarios, 'there is a good chance the spy is on this bus?'

'A very good chance,' said Jake.

Harvey nodded thoughtfully. 'We follow him,' he said at last. 'When we get the chance, we follow Francis and watch what he does, how he acts.'

'Good,' said Jake. 'Let's try that.'

'Hold on,' said Ellie. 'Let's not be short-sighted here. There are four of us. We could split into teams. Yes, follow Francis, but let's not take our eyes off the others. It could still be anyone, remember?'

'OK,' said Jake, looking back at Harvey. 'If you and Ellie take Francis, me and Dana will take the others, and then we've got our teams.' Ellie flashed him a smile, which Jake couldn't interpret. 'Is that OK?'

'Of course,' she said.

'Which brings us on to the other matter: what the hell happened to you in Atkinson's office?'

Ellie sucked in a deep breath. She explained to them how after she had been dismissed from Mr Walters' class, she had found Atkinson's office unoccupied. She had stood outside and waited for Atkinson's return, and when she did return she had been deep in conversation with Mr Harrison. She looked at them all. 'She made me promise not to say. I will tell you, but it can't leave this room.' They all signified compliance. 'The Legion is cutting the Level Twelve programme. This year will be the last. Atkinson said she would announce it to the school when they knew more about the replacement system.'

There was a pause while no one said a word. Then Harvey said, 'That's why Le Dich wants those files. He wants to know what he's got coming.'

'What do you mean?' Dana asked.

'He wants to get an idea of the people that are coming through the programme.'

'I believe it is more than that,' said Ellie. 'I believe he's trying to build a superior race.' She looked at Jake. 'Jasper was right. The Level Twelves are just for show. What it really comes down to is…'

'…mental and physical impairments,' finished Jake.

Ellie relayed to Harvey the conversation she had had with Jasper on the bus, the day before term started. 'What happens to everyone else?' said Harvey.

Ellie shrugged. 'We can be pretty sure of one thing.'

'What's that?'

'If Jasper *is* right and Laurie *is* still alive, she'll more than likely be here on Earth.'

The bus was approaching a checkpoint and they all crammed their faces to the small window to watch as they passed the barrier and entered the wetlands beyond. There were depth markers indicating the way the traffic should flow. Ellie watched as the discoloured water lapped up against the windowpane. She shuddered and tried to relax back into her seat.

The mood brightened when Mr Adlington went door to door, delivering breakfast. It was served in vacuum-sealed travel packs that oozed with condensation when their seals were broken. Ellie immediately burned the roof of her mouth with the sausages that she couldn't wait to allow to cool down properly. She blew fiercely on her beans whilst Harvey relayed for the others, what they had been doing in their metal works class.

'I wonder what you're building,' Jake said.

'I'm not sure, but it doesn't make a lot of sense.'

'How so?'

'Well, we only have so many parts and materials, and the thing we're building just seems to be getting bigger and bigger. It looks like a hatch or a door, but to what? We don't have enough parts for it to fix to anything else.'

Ellie blinked and considered as she observed their conversation. Then a thought occurred to her. 'Hey,' she said, dropping her fork in excitement. 'Remember on the first day he said he didn't want us to pay attention to anybody else, that we would work as a "whole unit" later on?'

'Oh, yeah,' said Harvey. 'He did say that.'

'Well, what if we're building a small part of something much bigger?'

'Something that connects to the other groups' projects?'

'Exactly.'

'But what?'

'All we know is that it has a hatch door built in.'

'Could it be a ship?' Jake said.

'I think it's too small to be a ship,' mused Harvey.

'Well, what then?'

'It's an escape pod,' said Ellie, mentally assembling the contraption in her mind. 'He's using us to build him an escape pod.'

Dana was on the edge of her seat, visibly thrilled. 'That settles it,' she said. 'Francis is our spy.'

Ellie turned to her. 'Didn't you know him before? You both came from St. Jude's, right?'

'No,' said Dana. 'Well, yes; but I mean, I didn't know him. I never attended any of his classes.'

'But you'd seen him around?'

'Never. I guess I'd heard of him but never had anything to do with him.'

They all stared through the plexiglass to the teachers' compartment in the front of the bus. Mr Francis had his back to them and he appeared to be in conversation with Mr Harrison, Mr Adlington and Mrs Ulsworthy.

'It's not him,' said Ellie. 'He's taken the place of someone who died in the disaster.' They all stared in wonder, jolting as the Aquabus found land beneath its wheels once again. They were passing through another checkpoint and gradually the scenery outside began to change from grey industrial skyscrapers to green hills and mountain houses. The holographic stewardess appeared again in the doorway and announced that they would be arriving at their destination in twenty minutes' time and to start preparing for their vaccinations.

They set about clearing away their waste from breakfast into the bins that pulled out from under their table. Mr Adlington made a cursory inspection of the compartments as the bus was making its final approach. When he entered Ellie's compartment he handed each one of them a key card. 'These are your room numbers,' he said. 'Keep them safe. When we arrive at the hostel, check into your rooms, and you'll have an hour before we meet in the reception area.'

'Where are we going after that?' Ellie asked.

'We're going to go off and have a look at some rocks,' said Mr Adlington enthusiastically. 'We'll take a lunch with us, because we'll probably be out all afternoon. Wrap up warm! We'll have dinner in the hostel when we get back.'

As the bus made its way down a dirt track towards an archaic cobbled building, Jake, Dana and Harvey all pushed their faces to the window to look out. Ellie was watching the other students in the other compartments. Everyone was doing likewise, even the teachers. Everyone, that is, except Mr Francis, who sat stock-still in his seat.

Ellie and Dana had a room to themselves and they made their way down to the east wing of the building. Jake and Harvey were on the other side, and when they separated, they all agreed to meet up with the rest of the group in an hour's time.

'This is nice,' said Dana as they entered and inspected the interior of their temporary lodgings. The walls bore ancient hangings, paintings and photographs. Some of the photographs were playing in a slideshow and depicted workers in and around the hostel grounds from generations past. The beds were laden with pillows and plump quilts. Ellie jumped onto a bed, flinging several of the more decorative pillows to the floor. She looked around at the pale-pink furniture with an expression of abhorrence. 'Isn't it nice?' Dana said again.

Ellie propped herself up on her elbows and looked out of the window. 'It's nice scenery,' she said.

Dana moved over to the window to have a look. 'Ellie?' she said.

'Uh huh?'

'Aren't you scared?'

'About what?'

'About this superior race idea? You know, Jasper's theory?'

Ellie looked at Dana thoughtfully. 'Sure, I guess. If Jasper is right, I can see why he'd be nervous.'

'And why is that?' Dana persisted.

'Because if they're building life that is free of disease and imperfections, he would feel that there was nothing he could do to get in.'

'Same with Laurie,' said Dana.

'Yeah,' said Ellie. 'I guess so. If we're right about all this.'

'And the same with you, no?'

Ellie looked at her sharply. 'Me?'

'You know, physical impairments,' said Dana, hovering a finger around her ear.

Ellie had flushed. She had never really thought of herself as being 'disabled' in any way. Her deafness had been with her as long as she could remember, so it was really just one of her characteristics; it helped to define her. She looked at Dana, who quickly averted her eyes back to the window. 'I'm sorry,' she said. 'I just thought—'

'Forget it,' said Ellie.

'Ellie?'

'I said, forget it.'

'But, Ellie?'

'What?'

Dana was pointing out the window. 'It's Mr Francis,' she said. 'He's leaving the hostel, look!'

Ellie jumped from the bed and joined Dana at the window. There, sure enough, was the figure of Mr Francis scuttling across the car park to the dirt track that would lead him out of sight and back to the main road.

'Come on,' said Ellie, 'now's our chance!'

Dana followed Ellie's already retreating form. All the students and teachers were using their hour's break to catch up on some rest, so the communal areas of the hostel were largely deserted. The dining hall was preparing for lunch, but otherwise the coast was clear, and Ellie and Dana dashed straight through the reception area to the car park. They shot across to the dirt track and began to sprint up it, blood and the excitement of the chase pumping through their veins, warming them.

It wasn't long before they could see Mr Francis ahead of them. They could see that the street widened as it opened into a small square, full of shops, cafés and weather hubs. They watched as Mr Francis entered an old cobbled building that had a sign outside, which read 'The Trump Card'.

Ellie and Dana drew closer and peered through the misty windows. Inside it was packed full of rowdy patrons, who drank merrily and appeared to be talking over each other constantly. Dana placed her hands over her ears to demonstrate to Ellie the level of noise.

'That's good,' said Ellie. 'No one will notice us.'

They pushed open the door and squeezed their way between the bodies that crammed the small bar. They made their way right to the back of the room until they reached a small booth. There was a partition of frosted glass between it and the next booth, which Mr Francis had entered.

'I can't see through the glass,' whispered Ellie. 'We're gonna need your ears.'

Dana kneeled on the cushioned bench and placed her ear close to the glass divide. 'He's meeting someone,' she relayed. 'He said, "Thank you for seeing me."'

Ellie nodded. 'And?'

'Something about having poor signal here,' went on Dana.

Dana listened carefully, but as she did so they were disturbed by a group of three women who advanced towards them, brashly proclaiming injustice at having the seats occupied by two kids. Ellie did her best to field the disturbance, while Dana did her best to hear what was going on next door. Eventually, however, the disturbance took its toll and Mr Francis left discreetly with a tall, thin man.

Seeing now that the booth had become empty on that side, the three women made their way to it, still broadcasting loudly.

'Come on,' mouthed Ellie through the din. 'They left. Let's get out of here.' Dana followed Ellie back through the over-filled bar to the outside street. Ice-cold sleet was beginning to fall from the sky, and Dana's head was lowered in solemnity. Ellie was about to say, 'Come on,' again and suggest making a dash for the hostel, when she noticed that Dana was crying.

'What's up?' Ellie asked. 'Don't worry about those women. They were drunk; they didn't know what they were saying.'

'I'm not crying because of them,' Dana sobbed. 'I heard them, Ellie. Before they left, I heard what Francis was saying.'

'What was it?'

Dana sniffed. 'It was the message from Le Dich, the bit that we didn't hear before.'

Ellie looked at her, agog.

'There isn't going to be any replacement programme for the Level Twelves,' said Dana. 'That must be something they just told Atkinson. There isn't going to be anything at all!'

'What do you mean?'

'After this year's Level Twelves, they're going to destroy the Earth.'

TEN

ELLIE AND DANA arrived back just in time to throw on some extra layers before joining the rest of the students at the hostel foyer. They had walked back slowly despite the sleet that had dripped from their hair and trickled down to the ends of their noses. They stood now in a solemn silence while everyone else stood about restlessly, waiting to be escorted by Mr Adlington back to the Aquabus.

Neither Harvey nor Jake could figure out what was the matter with them as Ellie and Dana fell into slow, disconsolate step behind the rest of the group, as it trudged over the stark moorland. Mr Adlington was delivering bright and cheerily on limestone and gritstone ridges, making small incisions in the rocks with a miniature drill. Ordinarily this was a pastime that Ellie would have relished, but as he collected the powder from the rocks into vials and placed the vials into a small case, insisting that the resulting tests would 'give us a real idea of the age of the rocks', Ellie stared at the scenery with scorn and gnawed at her fingernails.

Dana was equally uncommunicative, and neither would so much as talk to Jake or Harvey until they were making their way back to the hostel in the seclusion of their plexiglass cubicle. The light coming through the small porthole was all but extinguished now. Jake placed a hand over an overhead sensor, illuminating the space with a warm radiance.

'Is anyone going to tell us what's happened?' he asked, pulling off sodden gloves that turned inside out as they clung to his fingers.

Dana and Ellie exchanged a fatalistic look, then, with some effort, Dana began to explain how they had followed Mr Francis to the tavern, how they had tried to listen in on the conversation and how the women had interrupted them.

'What was he saying?'

'He was relaying the message from Le Dich,' said Dana.

'Who did he meet with?' Harvey said. 'Did you see?'

'Caught a glimpse,' said Dana. 'Tall and thin. No one we recognised.'

'So what was he saying to this guy?' Jake asked. 'Making his excuses for why he's not breaking into Atkinson's office right now?'

'Are we assuming this other guy has a Legion connection as well?' asked Harvey. 'Was it like some kind of progress report?'

'I don't know,' said Dana, her voice cracking slightly. 'I only heard Francis speak.' She swallowed and bristled as they gaped at her. 'Well, anyway,' she said, determinedly inspecting her nails and avoiding their eyes, 'we now know the end of the message.'

'Which is?' Jake and Harvey said together.

Dana faltered, but the electronic voice of Ellie's Speaking Aid piped up. 'They're going to destroy Earth,' she said.

For the next few moments Jake opened and closed his mouth like a goldfish gasping for life. Harvey studied her expression closely, as though he were waiting for her to crack up and start laughing, but Ellie only stared back at them, blankly.

'Wha… what?'

'It would appear,' she went on, 'that the Legion is cutting the programme and then after this year's Level Twelves they plan to destroy the Earth.'

'He said that?' Jake said, confirming.

Ellie looked at Dana, who was hiding behind a curtain of her hair. She caught Ellie's eye meekly and nodded. 'Yes,' she said, 'that's what he said.'

'We should talk to Harrison,' said Jake.

'What makes you trust him?' Ellie challenged.

'You're not still suggesting the spy could be anyone other than Francis, are you?' Harvey chimed in.

Ellie shrank back into her seat and used sign to say, 'I don't trust anybody.'

Harvey and Dana both looked at Jake. 'What did she say?'

'Nothing,' he sighed.

After they arrived back at the hostel, Ellie and Dana checked back into their room. Dana had been about to say something when Ellie picked up a towel and left the room. She could see that Dana was about to speak and she wouldn't like to hurt her feelings, but she couldn't face it right now. She just needed a minute to herself.

She marched across the hall to the female shower block and stood back from the showerhead while she waited for the water to heat up. Once she had got the water to the hottest temperature she could handle, she stepped in, turning her face up into the jet stream and scrunching her eyes shut against the blistering blast. Brown mud and filth collected in the water around her feet, and she watched in wonder as it spiralled round in circular sweeps before escaping down through the drainage hole. Steam filled the room as the hot water met with the cold air. She could not say for sure how long she had stayed in the shower, but when she emerged, Ellie's face tingled from the pummelling it had undergone and she sported red blotches from the heat.

Her fingers were wrinkled with the wet and, hugging a large towel around her shoulders, she skipped back across to the bedroom, leaving a trail of moist impressions upon the carpeted floor. Dana was sitting in front of the dressing-table mirror when Ellie entered, clasping her locket in her hand. In the reflection of the mirror, she saw Ellie spot this. 'I suppose it doesn't matter anymore,' she said. 'About Laurie, I mean. Not if they're gonna kill us all soon, anyway.'

Ellie dabbed at the wet strands of her hair and secured her Speaking Aid around her neck. 'If they're not gonna do it 'til after the exams, you still have a chance of

boarding the flight-to-freedom. You, Harvey and Jake.'
Dana grimaced and turned around just as there was a
knock at the door. 'Oh,' she said, 'speaking of, that'll be
them now.'

Still dressed only in towels, Ellie pulled open the
door. Harvey stammered nervously and Jake went purple
to the roots of his ears. 'Oh, er… hi, Ellie. We were…
well, er… Are you coming to dinner?'

'Dana and I will see you down there,' she said.
They nodded in unison but did not budge from the
doorway. 'So,' said Ellie, her eyes widening, 'bye-bye,
now.' She threw the door shut with a bang and looked at
Dana. Dana's head was lowered and her shoulders were
shaking; Ellie thought for a moment that she might be
crying again. She moved over to the little dressing table,
but when Dana looked up her eyes were wet with tears of
mirth. Ellie couldn't remember the last time she had seen
Dana laugh, and she threw her arms around her, rocking
gently back and forth on the stool as she joined in.

During their dinner Dana and Ellie kept a fairly low
profile. They sat quietly amidst a throng of excited chatter
from the other students. Ellie looked around at them all,
balancing a roast potato on the end of her fork. There were
representatives of different Level Groups on the trip, and
Ellie looked at the younger students, feeling as though she
might vomit into her plate despite the fact that these were
the first real potatoes she had tasted in years.

She looked from the students to the teachers' table. If
the message from Le Dich was true, were they all to die?
What was to become of Mrs Atkinson, Mr Adlington and

the older generations? What was to become of everyone she had ever met? Her sorrow and fear was not entirely selfless. She also played over the idea in her head that Dana had inadvertently planted: that she might be significantly enough impaired that she could be barred from Legion selection. Was Jasper's theory accurate? Had she effectively been sentenced to death?

Seemingly able to interpret this last thought, Dana put an arm around Ellie's shoulder. 'Do you really think we'd go without you?'

She had spoken soothingly, but something about her calm assuredness riled Ellie far more than she was expecting. 'Why wouldn't you?' she snapped.

Dana pulled her arm away as though she had been bitten. Her face creased in anxiety. 'What are you talking about?'

'Sorry,' said Ellie. 'But seriously, you have a chance to survive. Why would you not take it?'

Jake and Harvey leaned over with interest. It had been a while since either Dana or Ellie had said anything at all, and they were ready for some conversation.

'Because,' said Dana in a hushed tone, 'I'd rather die than live in a place of such limited moral code.'

'I'm sure we'll all be selected if we pass our Level Twelves,' said Harvey in an effort to appease everyone.

They all turned on him. 'Are you kidding me?' said Ellie. 'Why would I even bother with my Level Twelves given what I now know?'

'What I mean,' said Harvey, 'is if you don't try and pass, aren't you just making their decision easier?'

'I'm not playing their game, Harvey.'

'But you'd be giving them a more legitimate reason to exclude you.'

'Who cares?' cried Ellie. 'Who's gonna care what the reason was, after I'm dead?'

She could tell immediately from their expressions that she had drawn considerable attention to their circle. She hadn't realised that the Speaking Aid would interpret the violent fury that burned inside her chest and turn it into a verbal exclamation. She looked around at the faces that looked over at her and realised that this was exactly what had happened. She stood up abruptly and faced the teachers' table. 'I'm sorry,' she said. 'May I be excused?'

'Certainly,' said Mr Harrison as he got up, wiping his hands with a hot flannel. 'Everyone, please finish your meals. Ellie, let's go this way, together.'

He followed her into the reception area and silently indicated they should sit down. 'What's all this about, then?' He spoke briskly. He did not possess the same ability as Mrs Atkinson to sound concerned and caring. Rather, he sounded mildly irritated.

Ellie shook her head. 'Nothing,' she said.

Dana, Harvey and Jake had appeared in the doorway. 'I thought I told you to stay put and finish eating,' said Mr Harrison.

'We have something to tell you,' said Jake.

'I was hoping Ellie had something to tell me.'

'She won't, but we will,' said Jake.

Ellie glared at him. The intensity of her glare did not relax as she sat and watched them explain to Mr

Harrison their fear that the Legion was going to destroy the Earth after this year's Level Twelves, how the selection process bore little relation to the outcome of the exams and finally how Mr Francis may be a spy for the Legion, who was having his metal works class build him his own escape pod.

Mr Harrison listened to them open-mouthed as Dana related the conversation they had overheard in the tavern. 'This is a very serious allegation,' he said finally.

Ellie laughed a short and bitter laugh. 'We are very serious. You saw the message from Le Dich, same as Francis did. You should know our theories are actually based on something.'

'I knew there was someone else there,' said Mr Harrison quietly. 'You lot shouldn't be sneaking around after curfew.'

'Excuse me,' said Ellie, 'but I think you're missing the point. You don't get to call the shots anymore.'

The others stared at her incredulously. Even Mr Harrison looked unprepared for such brazenness.

'You need to make an announcement to the school,' Ellie went on.

'Oh, brilliant,' said Mr Harrison with a hollow laugh. 'Why? So that we can induce panic in every single student? It's bad enough with four; imagine if everyone knew what you lot know. We would have a nightmare on our hands if we lost control to that extent.'

'That's important to you, isn't it?' Ellie said. 'Control?'

Mr Harrison's eyes bulged with indignant amazement. 'I beg your pardon?'

'I wonder why,' said Ellie, 'when you have absolutely no control over what the Legion does.' She sighed and rose from her seat. 'Unless, of course, it is you who is the spy.'

'Where do you get that?'

'You and Francis were within minutes of each other, finding that message. You both argued about who should stay behind and carry out its instructions.'

Mr Harrison rose to his feet, and the two of them faced each other aggressively. 'I wanted to stay behind in order to identify the real spy,' he spat.

'Francis could say the same thing,' Ellie shot back.

'You'd better watch yourself, Miss Webster. I don't like your tone.'

'No,' said Ellie, 'you don't like *me*. I had never really appreciated the levels of prejudice that existed in the "adult" world, but I am beginning to appreciate it a whole lot more. I thought that bullying and discrimination was something that people might grow out of. God, how naïve of me. For all I know, you and Francis could both be spies, jostling for position in this so-called "society". I wouldn't join the Legion if you begged me, and as for my "tone", you won't have to hear it ever again.'

She tore the Speaking Aid from around her neck, holding it up in a clenched fist. 'This Speaking Aid is an invention of the lazy, which makes life easier for the listener, not the speaker. I have used sign language since I learned to walk, so why don't you do me a favour…' She threw the necklace to the ground and stamped on it with her heel.

'Miss Webster,' said Mr Harrison, 'you can expect to receive a fine for your blatant disregard of school property.'

Ellie signed something at Mr Harrison that he could not understand. He turned to the others. 'What did she just say?'

'She said, "Sue me,"' said Jake.

ELEVEN

THERE HAD BEEN a shift in the dynamics since the Peak District expedition had returned to Oakham. An irreversible change had been brought about following Ellie's dinnertime outburst and resulting conversation with Mr Harrison.

Both Ellie and Mr Harrison had sought out Mrs Atkinson at the first opportunity following their safe arrival back at school. Mr Harrison had been disappointed with the impartiality of her response and taken it upon himself to issue Ellie with a fine for damages to school property. Undaunted, Ellie successfully appealed the decision on the grounds that it was not the school's property but her own, and Mr Harrison's resentment of her was now on a gentle and constant simmer.

'We can't allow the students to start dictating terms,' he had said. 'She needs to be put in her place.'

'Stanley, you have no case with the Speaking Aid,' argued Mrs Atkinson. 'She bought it with her own money. Legally speaking, it is hers to do what she wants with.' They were outside, performing an evening patrol of the perimeter fence. Mr Harrison pulled his hood up over his head and shivered against the wintery chill. 'Why are you trying to catch her out?'

'You didn't see the way she looked at me,' said Mr Harrison. 'There was loathing in her eyes.'

'For goodness' sake, she was scared,' said Mrs Atkinson. 'She and her friends have uncovered some very disturbing things.' She raised a hand defensively as Mr Harrison's indignation began to boil over. 'How she discovered them is, I know, a contentious issue, and I certainly don't condone sneaking around and following people for the purposes of spying on them. That said, she had a suspicion, a suspicion you yourself shared.'

'I know,' he admitted.

'All I'm saying is I think we need to show these kids some leniency.' She spoke soothingly. 'Ellie, Jake and the other two.'

Mr Harrison offered a non-committal, 'Hmm,' for a reply.

'Ellie Webster has made a complaint to me, about you. She thinks that you don't like her. She seems to think also that you are prejudiced against her because of her disability.' Mrs Atkinson shone a torch through the school fence to some wild foliage as she spoke.

'That is absolutely absurd,' spluttered Mr Harrison.

'Is it? I hope so, because it is quite a serious allegation. I have you complaining to me about her and her complaining to me about you. What am I to do?' Mr Harrison looked for a moment as though he were trying to formulate an answer. 'I'm not actually asking,' said Mrs Atkinson. 'I know what I have to do, really, and that is to tell you both to grow up.' She pulled her torch away from the fence and looked at him. 'I shouldn't have to be saying this to you,' she said, and she shone the torch back at the path as they turned the corner of the school boundary.

Ellie sat in her treehouse with Jake. She hugged a thick parker round her waist and shuddered as the wind brought droplets of water down on her head from the leaves and branches above. She rubbed her nose with the back of her hand.

'Look, Ellie,' said Jake. 'Don't you think we could do this somewhere else? Somewhere warmer?'

'It's not safe,' she signed. 'Did you have any luck?'

Despite the cold and the damp, Jake couldn't help but look slightly pleased with himself. 'I did, as it happens,' he said. 'Not with Laurie, but the other thing.'

He pulled from his bag an old photographic print mounted on card. 'I had it enlarged at the library.' He sniffed, handing it to her.

Ellie grinned as she looked at it. 'Perfect.'

Jake shoved his hands deep into the pockets of his jacket and looked up at the evening sky. Through the misty veils of cloud, he could see the light of the moon partially shielded. He scanned the sky for the big star. At first he couldn't see it, but then he noticed it. It looked smaller than he remembered, though it was identifiable by its yellow, pitted surface. He squinted up at it in frowning consternation, raised a finger to it and positioned his arm like the barrel of a gun. Looking along his arm, his finger resting right over the star, he said, 'Ellie, can stars appear bigger and smaller at different times?'

Ellie, who was still inspecting the photograph he had given her, looked up to see what he was pointing at. 'What? What time is it?'

'Quarter to eight,' said Jake, dropping his arm and consulting his work pad. 'You're not seriously gonna go back there, are you?'

Ellie looked at him with a face that said, 'Come on, you know me better than that.'

He sighed and stifled a laugh. 'Yeah, I guess,' he said. 'I just don't understand why you would risk putting yourself in any danger.'

'Me and Harvey have a plan.'

'Oh, that's reassuring.' Jake laughed.

'He doesn't know he's suspected yet. I have to do this before he does.'

'Well, come on then,' said Jake. 'We'd better get going; it starts at eight, doesn't it? I'll walk with you to the hall.'

As they slid down to the earthen floor and started back to the school together side by side, Jake wondered whether he should take her hand but then thought better of it. He looked at her as they scuttled back over to their hole in the fence, but Ellie's face wore a set look of determination. She would be unshakable now. Jake thought about saying something, but Ellie held up her hand. She pointed to a far corner of the school grounds. Two shadowy forms could be seen shuffling around to the front entrance. One of them was shining a torch at the ground. 'Atkinson,' breathed Jake. Cautiously they ducked under their hole in the fence and sped over the tarmacked interior grounds to the open window of the teachers' canteen.

As the two teachers re-entered the hall, Mr Harrison straightened his collar and adjusted the robe around his shoulders. 'Do you suppose there's any truth to this theory, then? That Francis could be a spy for the Legion?'

Mrs Atkinson regarded him critically. 'I'm a strong believer in being innocent until proven guilty,' she said. 'So far nothing is proven. It is, as you say, only a theory.'

'What about this message from Le Dich?'

'What about it?' said Mrs Atkinson, looking up at the repaired patch of roof. 'It could be a hoax designed to panic us.'

'Is that what you really believe?'

She sighed and removed her dampened coat. 'The message starts with him saying that he'll be brief "in case it has fallen into the wrong hands", leading us to believe there is a spy among us that the message is intended for. However, he then goes on to reveal everything, including the sucker punch that he intends to destroy the Earth.' She made a weighing motion with her hands. 'The man is unhinged.'

'Unhinged enough to do something as crazy as destroy the Earth?' Mr Harrison said.

She shot him a contemptuous look. 'I am not going to let him panic me. That is what he wants.'

Mr Harrison scoffed but said no more.

'My staff are clean,' she went on. 'I've checked up on everybody.'

'Including Mr Francis?'

'Yes,' said Mrs Atkinson mordantly, 'and you.'

Mr Harrison stiffened and dusted his sleeve. 'So there is no spy?' he confirmed. 'Have you told Ellie and her band of brothers?'

Mrs Atkinson straightened her back. 'I can tell her now,' she said.

Ellie and Jake had reached the lift to the basement at the same time as most of the other students. Harvey had entered the lift with some of the other boys and held the door for her, but she shook her head. 'I'll see you down there,' she signed.

Harvey had got used to reading sign language a little better since the demise of the Speaking Aid. He nodded in understanding and let the door slide shut.

'Are you going to tell me what this plan of yours involves?' Jake asked after the lift had begun its descent.

Ellie shook her head and smiled. 'You'll see.'

'I'm not going to find out in the middle of the night, am I?'

'No!' She giggled.

'Promise?'

She nodded.

Jake played nervously with his fingers, then made an unexpected lunge with his hands, taking hers in his, much to his surprise as well as hers. She looked at him with curiosity, her head slightly tilted. Jake didn't have time to contemplate his next move before a voice behind him made him let go of Ellie's hands, startled.

'Mr Wilks!'

He looked over to the main entrance. Mr Harrison and Mrs Atkinson were making purposeful strides towards them. Ellie followed his gaze and groaned inwardly.

'Ellie,' said Mrs Atkinson. 'You know, I'm mindful that we haven't talked for a while. What a good thing I happened to run into you. Won't you come and sit down for a moment?' She indicated a door next to the lift. Ellie raised her hands to put together a response, but Mrs Atkinson interposed. 'I know you are probably eager to get off to your metal works class, but please, I won't take up too much of your time.' Ellie glanced at Jake. 'Mr Wilks can come, too,' said Mrs Atkinson, and she held open the door. 'Please.'

The four of them piled into the empty classroom, and Mrs Atkinson gestured for Ellie and Jake to have a seat. 'Are you still enjoying these classes?'

Ellie nodded quickly.

'Hmm,' considered Mrs Atkinson. 'I'm glad to hear it, though I would understand if you had stopped attending altogether.'

'Mr Francis is a good teacher,' signed Ellie. 'I'm learning.'

'Do you still believe he has you building him an escape pod, if such a thing is possible?'

'It wouldn't surprise me,' returned Ellie. 'I'm beginning to think that just about anything is possible.'

'But you still rate him as a teacher and attend his class?'

'Absolutely.'

'So what's the plan?' Mr Harrison cut in. 'You finish the class and steal the pod for yourself?'

Ellie clicked her fingers at him sarcastically, as though a cartoon lightbulb had appeared above her head. 'What a great idea.'

Mrs Atkinson looked at her colleague in silent exasperation, then turned back to Ellie. 'I wanted to talk to you about Mr Francis,' she said. 'I understand that you have some reservations about him, and if I'd heard what you've heard, I would probably feel the same way. However, I wanted you to know that since these concerns have been raised I have done a little digging of my own.' She perched on the edge of a desk. 'It is my duty as headteacher of this school.'

Mrs Atkinson stalled for a moment and Ellie nodded in encouragement. 'Well,' she said, 'I have been in touch with the Emergency Response Unit that assisted in the rescue at the St. Jude's disaster. I have been through the lists and the, er…' She cleared her throat. 'The casualties.'

'And?' Jake prompted.

Mrs Atkinson shot Jake a look, then looked back at Ellie, who was looking up at her expectantly. 'Everyone is accounted for,' she said. 'The Response Unit have identified our Mr Francis from the wreckage reports and Mr Francis has no association whatsoever with the Legion. He has never so much as left the Earth's orbit.'

'How do you know that?' said Jake.

'Because he has never owned an Interplanetary Pass,' she said, 'and he would never have been able to get through customs without one.'

'What about the tattoo?'

'Who knows?' said Mrs Atkinson, flicking a strand of hair away from her eyes. 'Perhaps he's a fan. What I can tell you is that any suspected Legion association must be a misinterpretation of the facts.'

Ellie considered for a moment then burrowed in her bag. She pulled out the photographic print Jake had given her in the treehouse. She looked at it again, as though to make quite sure, then handed it to Mrs Atkinson. 'Have I "misinterpreted" this?'

'What am I looking at?'

'Front row, six in from the left,' said Jake.

Mrs Atkinson's eye wandered over the image. It appeared to be an old school photograph. The words 'St. Jude's' were printed centrally and at the bottom. Underneath the heading was inscribed the names of all the teachers and students depicted. Mrs Atkinson put a finger on the front row and brought it across to the sixth figure from the left. She gave an involuntary gasp of surprise.

'What is it, Yvette?' asked Mr Harrison.

'Mr Francis,' she said distantly.

Mr Harrison glanced over her shoulder. 'Look,' he chortled, 'the photograph was taken nearly ten years ago. If it's a question of him looking different—'

'This is some difference, Stanley. I don't think skin colour tends to change with age.' Mrs Atkinson handed him the photograph and stood away from the desk, pacing slowly, hands on her hips. Mr Harrison did a double-take and brought the photo right up to his nose.

'You are quite the detective, Ellie,' Mrs Atkinson was saying. 'I suppose it wouldn't make any difference if I said that I would rather you didn't go to the metal works class this evening.' Ellie looked at her with a defiant stare. 'I didn't think so,' she said. 'Just promise me, you'll be careful.'

After having made the promise to Mrs Atkinson that she would, from now on, consult with her after every metal works session, she and Jake separated at the main staircase. 'I want regular updates,' Mrs Atkinson had said, 'and go easy; he can't know that we're on to him.' Jake stopped at the top of the first set of stairs and looked back at the main hall. He caught sight of her just as the lift doors closed, her face stony and brave.

The teams were already working industriously with their projects when Ellie reached the basement. Mr Francis was patrolling the cave, handing out hints and suggestions where necessary. 'Ellie,' he said brightly as she approached, 'good to see you again.'

Ellie smiled at him and made a show of apologising for being late, which Mr Francis waved away. 'Your group is waiting for you,' he said. Ellie scurried over to where Harvey, Nick and Doug sat poring over their collection of odds and ends.

'Why are there so many spare parts?' Doug was saying. 'There shouldn't be so many bits left over.'

'It's always the same,' said Nick, 'with anything like this. At least you can see a bit of structure to it now.'

Nick was right. Ellie stood and observed their partially built hatch door. She looked at Harvey. 'It's big,' she signed.

'Yes,' he agreed.

'Too big for a pod?'

'Hard to say,' said Harvey.

Doug and Nick looked up at them from the contraption on the floor. 'What are you two talking about?'

'Nothing,' said Harvey. He looked at Ellie and mouthed silently, 'Are you still up for this?' She nodded firmly.

There was little conversation for the remainder of the class. Ellie was watching the other groups with as much interest as she was giving to her own project. She tried mentally to piece the whole thing together but found this almost impossible. Some of the projects looked to be further along than others, and it was tricky even to gauge the overall dimensions of the completed assembly, such as it was.

Ellie stirred from her observations when the bracelet around her wrist signalled the end of the hour. She looked at Mr Francis who was saying, 'In the next session we can start looking at linking our projects together. We've come a really long way. You should all be very proud.'

Ellie kept her group there until most of the others had gone, asking them questions about what they thought it might be that they were building, and when the space had cleared somewhat, she led the way back to the lift. Mr Francis had retreated down one of the tunnels and

Harvey nudged her. 'Look,' he said, 'he's gone back to his office. Let's go.'

Ellie stopped short of the lift. 'I've left my bag behind,' she signed.

Nick and Doug looked from Ellie to Harvey. 'What's she saying?'

'She's forgotten her bag. I'll wait with her; you guys go on up.'

They shrugged and crammed into the lift with the last of the other stragglers.

Once the lift doors closed, Harvey moved over to join Ellie in the cave. He pulled a couple of lead pipes from the floor and handed one to her. 'Are you ready for this?'

'Wait,' she signalled.

'What for?'

'Aren't you curious to know what it is?'

'We know what it is,' said Harvey. 'It's a single-use escape pod. He's a scumbag, come on.'

'It can't be.'

'What? Come on, Ellie. Let's get it over with. He's a spy for sure. Whatever it is, it needs to be destroyed.'

'But it can't be a single-use escape pod,' she persisted.

'Why not?'

'Because this section has four seats.' She pointed to one of the other group's projects in the far corner of the room – a partially constructed floor and seating compartment.

Harvey lowered his piping and walked with her amongst the debris. 'Perhaps he's taking someone with him,' he suggested. 'Or maybe it's just standard kit and comes with four seats. He could still be using it alone.'

'Come on,' motioned Ellie, squatting down on the floor and inspecting some metal panelling. 'Help me pull this over to our door.'

'No,' said Harvey. 'I won't. We need to be quick, Ellie. We don't need to try and build it; we need to break it.'

Ellie giggled an uncertain giggle. 'Come on,' she implored.

'No!' shouted Harvey. 'If you're not going to do it, I will.' He raised the piping above his head and looked wildly around for something to bring it down on.

'I wouldn't do that if I were you,' came a voice from corner of the room. Mr Francis stood in the main cave, outside the tunnel marked WC. Harvey spun round to face him, still holding the pipe aloft. Mr Francis put up his hands as though trying to tame a lion. 'Let's all just take a minute here to think about what we're doing.'

'We know what you've been doing!' Harvey yelled. 'That's why we're here, right, Ellie?'

As Mr Francis inched nearer, he looked from Harvey to Ellie, who was rising slowly up from the floor.

'I don't know what it is you think I'm doing,' said Mr Francis, 'but I know you can lip-read, Ellie.'

She nodded.

'Right,' said Mr Francis calmly, 'then read mine—'

But before he could continue, Harvey made a spirited lunge at Mr Francis. Mr Francis ducked in time to miss catching a nasty blow to the side of the head. The weight of the lead pipe pulled Harvey off balance as his swing followed through. He tried to regain his footing, but before he could do so, Mr Francis was back up. With a deft and practised movement, Mr Francis threw an instinctive punch that caught Harvey smartly on the right temple. The boy crumpled and fell to the ground instantly. Mr Francis looked from the motionless Harvey on the floor to Ellie, but Ellie had picked up her bag and was backing away from him nervously.

TWELVE

ELLIE NEVER TOOK her eyes off Mr Francis while she was backing away from him. 'I don't want to hurt you,' he said, his hands raised in placation. 'I just can't have you destroying these projects. Believe me; it is in your own best interests.'

Mr Francis had crept into the middle of the cave by the time Ellie had reached the exit. He stopped right in the centre and dropped his arms, surrounded by the abandoned metal creations. He looked as though he were standing in the grave of a giant whale, with jagged metal sticking out around him at random angles like discarded bones. All of a sudden and quite unexpectedly, he crossed his legs and dropped to the floor. 'Can't we just talk a minute?' he said, looking up at her. Ellie felt this a curious tactic. She wondered if it were a trap. She had just witnessed Mr Francis executing the swift and assured violence of a trained soldier, though now he sat child-like and remorseful on the floor of the cave, gazing up at her beseechingly.

'Come and talk to me, Ellie,' he begged. 'Tell me what you think it is that's going on here.' Ellie hesitated, but despite her reservations she found herself moving back towards him. She was drawn by the overwhelming sense that this might be an opportunity to have some of her questions finally answered. She stepped gingerly over the fallen Harvey as she approached the centre of the cave. 'I'm sorry about your friend,' said Mr Francis, 'but he will be OK.' Without getting too close, she positioned herself in front of Mr Francis, sat down and folded her legs, placing her bag on her lap.

Mr Francis dithered as he wondered how to begin. 'You don't use your Speaking Aid anymore?' He smiled. Ellie shook her head. He placed his palms face down on the floor behind him and leaned back on them casually. 'Can you tell me why you wanted to smash up the projects we've been working on since the beginning of September?'

Ellie pulled her work pad and stylus from her bag. She opened a note and scrawled furiously over the screen for several moments, erasing and re-writing until she was satisfied with her composition. Eventually she looked up and slid the work pad over the floor towards him. Mr Francis picked it up and inspected the screen. He read aloud: 'The night the roof caved in, I saw what I knew to be *Pablucto Silvantes* among the bricks – I got out of bed to get it, but you had already found it – I followed you to a classroom and watched you play a message from Samuel Le Dich – I didn't see it all because Harrison came – I didn't know who the message was for, but

Harvey and my other friends thought it must be you on account of the fact that you have a Legion tattoo on your right arm – you then tried to stay behind from the school trip to fix the roof, as the message instructed you to – when Atkinson refused to allow that, me and my friend Dana followed you to a tavern in the Peak District,' Mr Francis's eyes widened in disbelief as he read on, 'where we saw you talk to someone about destroying the Earth.' He puffed his cheeks. 'Blimey O'Reilly,' he said.

Ellie gestured for him to hand back the work pad, and as he slid it back over the floor towards her, he said, 'The device was called *Pablucto Choloros*. I'd never used one before, but I knew what it was. It is a larger pebble than the *Silvantes*, an upgrade. It plays moving as well as still images.' Ellie nodded without interest, erased her previous message and started scribbling a new one. Again, she slid the work pad over the floor towards him when she had finished. Again, he read aloud: 'We knew we were building something in your class that was part of a bigger project – I started looking at the other groups and we decided that the project was too small to be a ship – however, some of the key features are the same.' He nodded, impressed. 'We thought you were building a single-use escape pod for when the Legion destroys the Earth – so we thought we would destroy *it*, then you wouldn't be able to escape.' He looked at her again, then rubbed his eyes.

Ellie indicated that she again wanted her work pad back. 'Hold on a minute,' said Mr Francis. 'Give me a chance to respond.' She relaxed her shoulders and indicated that he should go ahead. 'Right,' he said, 'I should have taken the *Choloros* to Atkinson straight away; that is where I made my first mistake. It was the middle of the night and I was curious. I just wanted to see what was on it.' Ellie nodded. *Understandable*, she thought. 'Well, when Harrison came, he thought the same as you: that I was playing a message from Le Dich that was intended for me. I tried to explain, but he is so pig-headed he wouldn't hear of any other explanation.' He grimaced. 'I wanted to stay behind on the Peak District trip so that I could keep an eye on the school and anyone trying to find those files for Le Dich. Harrison obliterated that plan, by probably trying to do the same thing. When it didn't work, I arranged to meet somebody there that I used to know. That'll be the man you saw me with in the tavern.'

Ellie used sign to ask, 'Who was he?'

Mr Francis slid the work pad back over to her but somehow seemed to interpret this question, anyway. 'He's someone I used to know in the Legion,' he said. Ellie flushed and pointed to his right arm. 'Yes,' admitted Francis. 'When I was your age, I passed my Level Twelves and boarded a flight-to-freedom, so help me God.' Ellie stared at him open-mouthed, unable to organise the thoughts that were mushrooming in her head. 'I was full of it,' went on Mr Francis. 'I had a good bunch of friends on the safe station. The tattoos were not part of any ritualistic ceremony or anything; they were just something me and my friends did. We thought they looked good.'

Ellie couldn't help but smile at this. It was so human.

'I worked as a mechanic until I was eighteen. I had a decent salary, I was young and there was no disease. Life was beautiful.'

'So what happened?'

Again, Mr Francis interpreted the question without her having to write it down. 'Six years,' he said. 'I'm ashamed to say it now, but I was there six years before I realised what was going on.'

'What was going on?' Ellie scribbled.

'There were kids I knew at school before the Level Twelves, here on Earth – kids that didn't make Legion selection. I didn't really stop to think about it at the time, but one day it just dawned on me: they can't all have had bad academic records.'

'The kids with physical disabilities?' Ellie wrote.

'Yes,' said Mr Francis.

'Kids like me?'

'Sure,' said Mr Francis. 'Kids with any kind of physical or mental impairment.'

'How is this tested?'

'In interviews and medical examinations after the Level Twelves.' Ellie blinked at him. 'Yeah,' he said with a wry smile, 'they don't tell you about that, do they?'

'So what is the point of the Level Twelves?'

'It's just a filtering process,' said Mr Francis with a sigh. 'It's one of the three stages of the examinations. You have to pass a level of intelligence, prior to the other tests, but it's the only one they tell you about. You need to pass all three to make the cut.'

Ellie shook her head in disbelief, scribbled something on her work pad and held it up for him to see. 'If they were just honest about it from the start, it would save a whole lot of pain, I think. At least people would know their limitations and not be encouraged to believe in something that can't exist for them.'

'People like you?' asked Mr Francis.

'I don't have limitations,' countered Ellie.

Mr Francis laughed. 'You know, I think you're right, and that is exactly why I defected. On Earth people are encouraged to believe that they are created equally. The Legion doesn't subscribe to this belief, but they needed the Earth for their recruits – initially, anyway. Le Dich and the founders of the Legion would have Earth believe they share their values merely in order to get what they want.'

Ellie's heart was pounding and her fingers trembled, but she gripped her stylus hard and wrote, 'So what's happening now?'

'They're done with us,' said Mr Francis simply. 'Le Dich wants to shut the door to further recruits.' He leaned forward. 'The first child died in infancy last year and they got scared. That's the truth of it. They blame Earth and the programme for the spread of infection. This is why I believe they want to destroy it. They'd see it as cleaning up after themselves.'

'Atkinson thinks the threat of destruction is a bluff to panic us.'

Mr Francis gave a harrumph as he read this last statement on Ellie's work pad. 'They could be trying to panic us,' he said, 'but I'm sure they intend to do it.' He pushed the pad back to her and Ellie looked around the room, embittered.

Finally, she picked up the work pad and wrote, 'If it's not an escape pod, what is it?'

Mr Francis smiled. 'It's called a "Paddle",' he said with unconcealed delight. 'It needs to be piloted like a ship, but it is designed to absorb and deflect blasts. It is shaped like a big teardrop.' He outlined the shape with his hands as he spoke. 'They are built to withstand tremendous shock and pressure. They've been used in ocean planets for deep-sea voyages, as well as for surveillance and many other missions. They're really versatile.'

'I've never heard of them,' stated Ellie. 'What do you intend to do with it?'

'I'm going to deflect the blast from the safe station and save the Earth,' he said succinctly. 'Want to come?'

Ellie's eyes widened, but she was still not ready to trust him. She must not allow herself to get carried away. She returned to her business-like line of enquiry. 'When did you defect?'

'I was nineteen and with three of my friends, we took off in a Bacca.'

Ellie's face did little to disguise her ignorance of this word. Mr Francis laughed and hastened to expand. 'A Bacca is a light exploratory craft, generally used for interplanetary deliveries.'

'And what did you do?'

'Over the next thirty years we developed what we called a "resistance programme" unbeknown to the

Legion. We still operate without their knowing much about us. You see, we are not at war with the Legion; we want as little to do with them as possible, if truth be known.'

'What do you do?'

'We constructed a fleet of four vessels, one each. They were similar to the Baccas but designed and built by us, so superior in quality, in my opinion.'

'What are they called?'

'The Revelry fleet,' he said with pride. 'We have Revelry One, Two, Three and Four. I pilot Revelry Two.'

Ellie looked at her work pad and began typing rapidly.

'You won't find any information about it on there,' he said. 'Our Revelry resistance is little known to anyone but our own growing population. We come to Earth after the Legion has absconded with their recruits and we offer a new life to those who didn't make Legion selection.'

Ellie gazed at him incredulously and composed another question for him on her work pad. 'Who *are* you?'

'My name is Alexi Carter,' he said. 'I volunteered for transportation to Earth at the time of the St. Jude's disaster. It was the belief of the resistance that the Legion was severing ties with Earth, and I took the place of Derek Francis when he sadly lost his life. So you are right in thinking I am a spy, but perhaps not quite in the same way as you had in mind.'

'Do you think there is a spy for the Legion here at Oakham?' Ellie asked.

Alexi Carter nodded grimly. 'I do.'

'Is it Mr Harrison?'

He shook his head and sucked in his bottom lip. 'I don't think so. He's obstinate and annoying, but not a spy.'

'Who then? I can't imagine it being any of the other teachers.'

'Perhaps you're looking in the wrong places, Ellie,' said Alexi Carter.

'What do you mean?'

'It's not a teacher.'

'Who then?'

'It's likely to be someone who came in with the lot from St. Jude's, someone you didn't know before. Just like me. Do you know anyone who claims to have been in that disaster?'

Ellie faltered, wondered whether she should let on; then she wrote, 'My friend Dana, but it couldn't be her.'

'Dana Humphries?' guessed Alexi Carter. Ellie nodded and Mr Carter chuckled. 'I should say not.' He laughed. 'I know her sister, Laurie. I'm glad you have a connection to her. Laurie will be relieved.'

Ellie brightened. 'You know Laurie? We've been trying to find her for months.'

'Well, you won't have much luck down here! Laurie's on Altarc.'

'Altarc?'

'Our very own safe station,' explained Mr Carter. 'Altarc is home.' He spoke slightly wistfully and dropped his chin. Ellie couldn't be certain what he said next, but it looked something like, 'I am looking forward to going home.'

Ellie was starting to feel reassured of Alexi Carter's trustworthiness. It all fitted and it was too much to invent on the spot. After one final struggle against the last few ounces of doubt, she made up her mind to believe him.

'Not to worry,' he was saying, 'if you don't know anyone else from St. Jude's; it'll be a case of going through the lists with Atkinson.'

'Wait!' Ellie put up her hand to halt him. 'Of course I know someone else. He must be from St. Jude's. We never talked about it, but I only ever saw him after that.'

Ellie had been signing this last thought, and Mr Carter looked at her critically, trying to understand. 'Have you thought of someone else?' he asked.

'Yes.' Ellie nodded emphatically.

'Who?' said Mr Carter.

Ellie swung around to point at the spot where Harvey lay motionless, but the patch of floor he had occupied was now deserted. Harvey was no longer there.

THIRTEEN

A LEXI CARTER'S FACE was contorted with angst as he and Ellie made a frantic search of the basement floor. 'He could still be down here,' he called out as he tore up and down passageways, turning over boxes and rubble in every room he came to. Ellie threw up her hands in a gesture of hopelessness as Mr Carter dashed past her. She had never seen him like this before. *He's being himself now*, she reasoned. Mr Francis was gone.

'He's been watching me this whole time,' Mr Carter said. 'It makes sense, I suppose. Le Dich was smart to send him.' He was talking more to himself now and Ellie stood, looking at him with her arms folded, shaking her head. 'I suppose you can't desert the Legion and expect them not to keep an eye on you,' he muttered. He looked at Ellie and pushed up the glasses that were slipping down the bridge of his nose. 'Whose idea was it to destroy the projects, his or yours?'

Ellie considered this. She didn't want to believe that Harvey could really be a Legion spy, but she knew full well that it was his idea. Her expression seemed to translate this, and Mr Carter said, 'Of course it was. It all makes sense, but how did he know what we were building?' Ellie stared at him, wondering if he was really in want of an answer to this last question. 'No matter,' he said at last. 'We can't hide down here forever, can we?' Ellie shook her head and wondered what was going to happen next.

Mr Carter pushed open the lift door and jumped inside. He waved for Ellie to join him, and as they rose to ground level, her mind went back over the times she had shared with Harvey. She saw his movie-star smile grinning at her; she saw his dark, prominent eyebrows regarding her and his chiselled cheekbones completing a face that was now – rather obviously, it seemed – too perfect. He had liked her. He wasn't so good an actor that he could fake liking her to such an extent. Still, she considered, he had forged a friendship with her based on some ulterior motive. She had provided him with the excuse he needed to discredit Francis. She felt sick to the stomach, and as the lift came to a stop she and Alexi Carter stepped into the main hall, both sporting expressions of matching hostility.

They made their way to the first staircase. It was only when they reached the top that they realised they were each heading in different directions. They looked over their shoulders at each other as though they were bounded by an invisible tether that had suddenly constricted. 'Where are you going?' Mr Carter said. Ellie pointed towards the boys' dormitory where she knew

Jake would be. 'We can't go and see your friends now,' he said. 'Come on, we'll catch Mrs Atkinson if we go now.' But Ellie shook her head with absolute conviction. 'Come on, Ellie. I need you with me to verify my story. She might not believe me.'

Ellie looked at him with staunch determination and signed, 'I'm not going anywhere without my friends.'

Mr Carter's face was, at first, a mask of puzzlement. His puzzlement cleared when she made to unpack the work pad from her bag. He waved for her to stop. 'That's alright,' he said. 'I have a pretty good idea what you're saying; my God, you're stubborn.' Ellie grinned at him, flattered. 'OK,' he said, 'round them up and meet me in Atkinson's office, will you?' Ellie nodded happily, turned on her heel and made a dash for the common room.

When she threw open the door, she was surprised to find the room fairly busy. She skimmed over the chatting faces until she saw Dana sat at a table in the corner, the curtains of her hair drawn in front of her face as she looked down at her mini work pad journal. Further inspection revealed that Jake was sitting across from her. He had his back to the door and appeared to be hunched over his own work pad. Ellie decided quickly that she must shelve the questions she had as to why Dana was in the boys' common room in the first place. She would only find herself the recipient of the very same question. Besides, her news could not wait. She ran over to them and plunged down into a seat on the sofa.

'Ellie,' said Jake in surprise. 'What are you doing here?'

Ellie frowned and hit him on the shoulder with the back of her hand.

'Sorry,' he said, 'I didn't mean…' He stopped. Ellie was looking at him with one of those unfathomable expressions that he recognised so well. 'What is it?'

Brimming with anticipation, she cracked her fingers and signed, 'You're never gonna believe what's happened.'

When Mr Carter rapped on the door to Mrs Atkinson's office, he was slightly taken aback to be received with familiarity and warmth. 'Come in, come in.' She smiled. 'Please, have a seat.' She gestured towards one of the chairs that stood before her grand mahogany desk and moved over to a receding cabinet that was built into the wall of the room. 'I was just about to have a nightcap.' She giggled flirtatiously. 'Can I procure something for you?'

Alexi Carter stammered, thoroughly caught off guard. 'Well,' he said, 'I ought not to, really.'

'Oh, but of course you will,' insisted Mrs Atkinson, decanting a golden liqueur into round mottled glasses. 'You will because we have so much to discuss.'

'Well, you're right about that,' said Alexi Carter.

'Of course I'm right,' sang Mrs Atkinson, stirring the liqueur with a long, twisted spoon and turning to him with an outstretched arm. 'Here,' she said. 'Here's to you.'

Mr Carter looked up at her from his seat and took the glass. 'Thank you,' he said. He sniffed at the liquid tentatively. 'This must have cost you a fortune,' he said. 'Where did you get it?'

'From my husband,' said Mrs Atkinson, sitting down behind her desk and gently agitating the glass under her nose. 'It was an anniversary present.'

Mr Carter looked thunderstruck. 'You ought to save it for a special occasion,' he said.

'If I were to do that,' said Mrs Atkinson, 'it would stay in its bottle for ever and ever, never released; and what a waste that would be.' She fixed him with a hypnotic stare from over her glass. 'Go ahead, drink.'

Jake and Dana were gaping at Ellie as she relayed to them the news that Mr Francis was in fact Mr Alexi Carter, that he was part of a resistance that gave sanctuary to those left by the Legion and that he had knocked Harvey unconscious after they had threatened to destroy the Paddle. They digested the news without interruption that Ellie and Mr Carter had concluded that Harvey must be the Legion spy. They watched her explain that just as she had made this realisation, they noticed that Harvey had disappeared.

There was an uncomfortable silence while Ellie waited for them to react. They exchanged a worried look, as they both thought the same thought. It was Jake who spoke first. 'Ellie,' he said, 'have you considered that this might all be part of some elaborate hoax?' She frowned and sank back in the sofa, but she gestured for him to explain. 'Well,' he said, 'it's just that: what if Harvey isn't a spy at all and he's just been assaulted by someone who he thought was? And what if he came round and saw you being convinced that he was the traitor? Do you know what I mean? You were his ally. You would have betrayed him, in his eyes; he probably freaked out. He could just be in hiding now.'

Ellie uncrossed her arms and patiently signed, 'I hear what you're saying and I would probably rather believe that, but I honestly don't think that's what's happening.'

'Why not?' Dana asked.

Ellie looked Dana right in the eye and signed, 'Because he knows Laurie.'

Mrs Atkinson watched as Mr Carter gave in to temptation, saluted her with his glass and drank deeply from it. She smiled and replaced her glass on the desk. 'Tell me, what should I call you now?'

He looked at her, uncertain what game it was that she was playing. 'I beg your pardon?' he said.

'Well, I can't rightly call you Mr Francis anymore,' she said. 'Not now that I know he was a black man who died in the St. Jude's disaster.'

'Ah,' said Mr Carter, comprehending.

'So,' she said in a voice that just hinted at an inner hostility, 'what is it that I should call you instead?'

'Carter,' he said. 'Alexi Carter.'

'Progress,' Mrs Atkinson smiled, 'at last.'

'You know, I can explain all this,' said Mr Carter.

'Oh, all what?'

'My reasons for secrecy,' he said. 'What I've been doing here at Oakham.'

'Can you? Well, you'll have to be quick about it; you'll be incapacitated soon enough.'

Mr Carter looked from Mrs Atkinson to the glass in his hand, and a rising sensation of fear bubbled up inside his chest.

Jake had protested a little more against the validity of Alexi Carter's claims than Ellie had deemed appropriate, but Dana was now of a one-track mind. 'I want to see him,' she said.

'It might not be true,' said Jake. 'I mean, hopefully it is, but we should be careful.'

'He's with Atkinson,' signed Ellie. 'He should be explaining everything to her. He wants us to meet them in her office.'

'Incapacitated?' said Alexi Carter.

'I'd say you've got about two minutes, tops.' Mrs Atkinson smiled.

Jake was still uncertain and preferred to reserve judgement, but Dana was already on her feet and leading the way to Atkinson's office. She walked so briskly that Ellie and Jake struggled to keep pace with her. As they turned the corner that put them within sight of her office door, there was the sound of a crash from within. Dana and Jake looked at each other fearfully.

'What's going on?' Ellie asked.

'It sounds like he's killing her,' said Jake, and he sprinted to the door, flinging it open dramatically. Ellie and Dana followed and halted at the threshold, just behind him. All three of them looked down at the figure of Mr Alexi

Carter, who appeared to have fallen backwards off his chair. Fragments of broken glass lay all around him and in his beard. His eyes stared up at them in a frozen picture of terror. Slowly, they tore their gaze away from this spectacle and in perfect unison brought their heads up to the unperturbed Mrs Atkinson, who still sat on the other side of the desk, holding her glass between the long, elegant fingers of one hand and running the fingers of her other hand through jet-black hair. 'Good evening,' she said.

Mrs Atkinson was, on the whole, rather pleased with her incarceration of Alexi Carter. As such, she was reluctant to hear arguments that the man might not only be innocent but also be the head of a freedom-fighting movement that fought for the custody of abandoned and often very poorly children. She held a hand to her head as she, Jake, Dana and Ellie stood over the fallen Carter and debated the various possibilities. 'I've never heard of any such resistance,' Mrs Atkinson was saying. 'As far as I'm aware, there is just the Legion and us.'

'I have a question,' said Jake. 'If the Legion is run by such a psycho, then why is there a programme in place to send us there in the first place?'

'Le Dich is just one man,' said Mrs Atkinson. 'The Legion is by all accounts something to aspire to.'

'Whose accounts?' put in Dana. 'We never see testimonials from those that have gotten in. We've never even seen so much as a photograph of the safe station.'

'It's a life without disease or famine,' she said humbly. 'It's an idea, a life after this.' She gestured to the room in general. 'You have to believe in it.'

'You have to believe in it before you can see it,' Jake confirmed. 'Maybe that's not such a good idea.'

'Maybe it's the perfect idea,' said Mrs Atkinson. 'The more we see, the less we seem to know.'

'This is ridiculous,' said Dana.

Ellie had walked around to behind Mrs Atkinson's desk and was inspecting the bottle of golden liqueur. She watched them all as the debate got more and more heated. Finally, she brought her fist down upon the desk with a thud that made everyone turn around.

'I believe that Mr Carter is who he says he is,' she signed. 'I have heard his explanations and he has convinced me. For those of you who are still undecided, there are a couple of ways we could prove it. One: finish the metal works construction. We'll soon know if it's a "Paddle", an escape pod or anything else.' There was quiet while Jake slowly translated Ellie's message into words.

'And the other way?' he asked.

'We find Harvey.' She moved around to the front of the desk and pointed at Mr Carter. 'What have you given him?'

'It's a mild tranquiliser,' said Mrs Atkinson. 'He should be fine in a couple of hours.'

Ellie nodded and communicated directly with Jake in sign language for a few moments. 'We're going back to the basement floor,' he said. 'Ellie and I will start trying to put this thing together downstairs. You two, try and bring him round as soon as possible. Dana will want to talk to him about her sister; that'll help verify his story. Then, when he's fit enough, we'll need his help with the construction.'

Mrs Atkinson looked at them both. 'I'll go along with this plan,' she said, 'but I'll send you some recruits to speed up the build. Meanwhile, I'll announce early closure of the school for the Christmas break.'

As Dana and Mrs Atkinson moved Mr Carter into the recovery position, Jake and Ellie left the office and began the walk down to the basement floor. There was an eerie sense of disquiet as they moved down to the main hall and across to the ancient lift. They both felt nervous, though neither liked to admit it. Ellie felt deeply disturbed by the disappearance of Harvey and struggled against the last flickering doubts she had at the back of her mind that she had indeed got it all wrong.

As they entered the lift, Jake said, 'I'm quite looking forward to seeing what you've been doing all this time.'

Ellie smiled a self-conscious smile and signed, 'Get ready to be impressed.'

When the doors slid aside and they stepped out into the majestic cave, Ellie scanned the area. It looked, however, just the same as when she and Mr Carter had left it. Jake strode purposefully over to the abandoned collections of metal. 'Which one is yours?' Ellie led him over to her hatch door and proudly indicated the finer details that she had painstakingly undertaken during that evening's session. 'Well, at least it looks like a door,' he offered. 'Some of these things, you can't tell what they're supposed to be. I mean…' He hesitated, noting the worried look on her face. 'Yet,' he said. 'You can't tell what they're supposed to be yet. I'm sure we can make sense of it.'

Ellie went from project to project, collecting instruction manuals. She placed them all down in the centre of the cave like the collection of evidence in a police station. Then she looked from the paperwork to Jake with such an expression of anguish that he couldn't help but laugh. 'Don't worry,' he said. 'One step at a time.' He picked up a single manual from the collection and said, 'Boarding ladder. That looks easy, where's that?' They searched the wreckage until Ellie's eyes fixed upon a collection of rungs in her own project box. She seized on it and offered it to him. 'This looks as though it connects to your door. Why don't we start with that?' suggested Jake.

They worked busily at the boarding ladder for the next half hour, fixing it to the exterior hull, just beneath the hatch. They worked avidly, sufficiently distracted that all their anxieties and other concerns were shortly pushed back to the furthest recesses of their minds.

It had already been late when they began and their energy was soon running low. Jake made a slip with a wrench, catching his finger a smart blow. He yelped and sucked on it sorrowfully. Ellie took his hand in hers to inspect the damage. It didn't appear to have broken the skin, but it looked as though there would be swelling and potentially quite a nasty bruise. She blew on his finger soothingly. Then, suddenly and without warning, she let go his hand, signalled that he'd be fine and stood up to move over to the wall of the cave.

'Hey,' he said, 'where are you going?'

She slumped down against the far wall, resting her back. Jake stood up and moved over to join her. 'We're tired,' she signed. 'We'll only start making mistakes now.'

Jake nodded. 'So shouldn't we go back upstairs?'

Ellie shook her head very firmly. 'Atkinson will be sending reinforcements soon. I'm not going to leave until someone else gets here. I have to guard it in case Harvey comes back.'

Jake shuffled into position next to her. 'You really think this story of Carter's is gonna check out?'

She rested her head against the wall and looked at him sideways on. 'I have to believe it.'

'So does Dana,' said Jake. 'So do we all, come to that.'

Ellie blinked slowly, then touched her fingers to the front of her neck so that she could feel the vibration of her vocal cords. She didn't like trying to speak. She was self-conscious about it, but she looked at him nonetheless and slowly said, 'You like Dana, don't you?'

Jake was startled. He had never known Ellie to speak before. He had only ever heard her voice when she had been laughing. He looked her in the eye. 'Yes,' he said, 'I like her. I didn't at first, but I made an effort because you wanted me to.'

'Because I...?' She faltered.

'Yes,' he said. 'Because you asked me to. There's nothing more to it than that.'

She moved her hand from her neck and placed it in his. She rested her head against his shoulder and closed her eyes in silent serenity. *Anything else would be a misinterpretation of the facts*, she thought to herself.

FOURTEEN

Ellie didn't know how long she had been asleep, but when she awoke she saw that they were still lying on the floor of the cave. The artificial light from the rafters above made it impossible to measure time, but in the time since they had drifted off and now, they had had blankets tucked over them and pillows placed under their heads. Mr Adlington and Mr Harrison stood among the semi-constructed metal works, blowing into Styrofoam cups and chatting indistinctly.

Ellie disentangled herself from the blankets she was swaddled in and rose to her feet. She looked around at the metal bones. There was evidence of marked progress and she rubbed her bleary eyes with the palms of her hands.

'Miss Webster,' said Mr Adlington with a warm smile. 'Welcome back to the land of the living.'

Ellie approached the two teachers and asked, 'What time is it?'

'It's just a little after 8.30,' said Mr Adlington, consulting his wrist in a business-like manner.

'Where are Mrs Atkinson and Dana?'

'Mrs Atkinson is holding an assembly to finish the term early. I believe your friend Miss Humphries is in Mr Fr... Mr Carter's office,' he corrected himself. 'They evidently share some mutual acquaintances.'

'Have you done all this?' She indicated the adjoining materials on the floor.

'Well, we can't take all the credit,' said Mr Adlington. 'Mr Carter has worked through most of the night. That is, since his faculties have been restored.'

'It seems we had him all wrong, this Mr Carter,' said Mr Harrison.

'We?' Ellie signed.

Mr Harrison shuffled his feet in uncomfortable silence and Mr Adlington said, 'Won't you have some breakfast? We've brought down some supplies. They're in the office. You two are going to need your strength today.'

'You mustn't, on any account, go upstairs,' said Mr Harrison. 'It could confuse the other students. Someone will send for your personal belongings later.'

'No problem.'

Ellie looked back over towards Jake, who was still out for the count. Smiling inwardly, she moved over to the passageway marked 'Office'. She thought of the first time she had set foot in here, how she had not been able to find the light switch and how she had crept fearfully down the tunnel in the dark. She took that same tunnel now with a confident and self-assured stride.

Stopping outside the office door that still had 'Mr Francis' carved into a wooden mount, she knocked and waited. A moment later the door was opened and there stood Dana, looking more alight with energy than Ellie had ever seen her before. 'Oh, Ellie,' she exclaimed, throwing her arms around her in a welcoming embrace. 'It's all true! He knows Laurie for sure. He's been telling me all about her. She works on Altarc and is involved with training in first aid and pilot training.' Ellie grinned and gave Dana a thumbs-up. She turned to Mr Carter, who was sitting behind his desk with a cold flannel draped over his forehead. She signalled that she would like some coffee. 'Of course,' he said. 'Can you remember how to do it?'

Ellie moved over to the antique coffee grinder and began decanting beans from a bag into the funnel at the top. As she waited for the water to heat up, she pulled a pastry from a basket on the desk and inspected the collection of artefacts that littered the small room. 'Are you looking for anything in particular?' Mr Carter said. Ellie made the sign for 'booklet'. Mr Carter dabbed at the cold compress on his head. 'Sorry?'

'She wants an instruction manual for the Paddle,' interpreted Dana. 'She wants to see what she's building.'

'Ah,' said Mr Carter. 'You know, I don't think it came with one. I ordered the lot in parts, at various online auctions. That's why we have manuals for the individual projects, but not one for the whole unit.'

Ellie sighed and poured hot water over the ground coffee, watching, fascinated, as the machine transformed the clear running liquid into the brown, sweet-smelling coffee that trickled slowly out into a jug on the hot plate.

'It shouldn't be much longer, anyhow,' he said. 'You lot have done most of the hard work. It's pretty much a case of sticking it all together now. I'll come and give you a hand, then I think Atkinson will be down later to talk to us, once she has dealt with the situation upstairs.' He got unsteadily to his feet and removed the flannel from his head.

Ellie looked at him doubtfully and signed, 'Are you OK?'

Mr Carter chuckled as he recognised the concern in her face. 'She did a bit of a number on me,' he said, 'but I'll be alright.' He staggered to the door and held it open for Dana and Ellie. 'Come on,' he said, 'back to it.' Ellie thrust another pastry into her mouth and another into the pocket of her cardigan before leaving.

Jake was still snoozing when they got back to the central cave, and Ellie chucked a pastry onto his blanket as though it were raw meat through the bars of a lion enclosure. She moved over to the circular gathering in the middle of the cave and watched as Mr Carter addressed them all on the next stages of the construction. 'There are three main parts of exterior and six of us,' he said. 'Ellie, you'd better wake up your buddy.' They looked at Jake and laughed. 'These two tepee-shaped domes are the main body. They're gonna meet in the middle on top of this floor section in the shape of a big water droplet. At the back, there will be a space for the hatch door, which will be fitted last. The next bit is going to involve holding things in place, welding and pinning. It may take the best part of a couple of hours, but after that it'll—'

A sound at the entrance of the cave made him stop. Everybody looked over. Ellie followed their gazes, which all rested on the lift doors. There was a light on, indicating that the lift was in use.

'Who's that?' Dana said.

Mr Adlington glanced at his wrist again. 'I didn't think Yvette would be finished yet,' he said.

'No,' agreed Mr Harrison. They all watched as the light on the lift went from red to green and the doors slid back.

Ellie flushed with rage, Dana caught her breath and the three men bristled as Harvey stepped from the lift into the cave. He walked towards them with soundless steps, stopping a good twelve feet from them, his hands at his sides. *He looks different*, Ellie considered. *Less casual*. He wore a tunic-style jacket that was tied with a belt around his waist and his feet were bare. He looked as though he were a martial arts expert. His hair, moreover, was cropped neatly to his head, and his face was bright with cleanliness.

'Hi, Ellie,' he said in a dry monotone. 'How are you getting on with that?' He pointed at the rounded metal tepees.

Ellie was quietly fuming and declined to respond.

'Oh, come on,' said Harvey, 'don't be like that. I'm sure you would be further along if I hadn't been there sabotaging your progress as you went.' He looked at Mr Carter. 'She really is quite intelligent, you know.'

'You're not telling me anything new there,' said Mr Carter. 'I know all about it.'

A strangled cry of fury burst out from Jake, who had risen to his feet when he had seen Harvey entering. He now ran and hurled himself at Harvey, leading with his shoulder. Harvey watched disinterested as Jake fell through him and landed on his shoulder with a yell of agony. 'Yes,' he said coolly. 'It's not hard to see who has the brains in this particular outfit.' He looked at Jake. 'I expected better of you, Wilks. You might have had a promising career aboard the safe station. Too bad.' He looked again at Ellie and the rest of the group. 'As Jake here has helped me to demonstrate, I am not actually with you right now. I am, in fact, in the safe station and appearing to you by holographic link.'

'What is it?' Mr Adlington asked.

'I beg your pardon?'

'The message, whatever you've come to say.'

'Of course,' said Harvey. 'As you will remember, the pebble that struck the roof of the school last month contained a message from my father.'

'Your father?' Dana said in a voice of absolute disgust.

'That's right,' said Harvey, 'though you may know him better as Samuel Le Dich. The message was a crude attempt to scare you all into a frenzy and induce a situation where the school would have to close. It actually worked better than I thought it would, to be fair, and by some sleight of hand we have found ourselves in exactly that situation. Atkinson has just made her announcement upstairs.'

'Why did you need the school to close?' said Mr Harrison.

'In order to pass a vote,' said Harvey. 'A vote as to whether or not we should cut our losses and sever our ties from the Earth permanently. We needed the school to close before we could count the vote, so originally this wasn't going to happen until after the exams. With the school closing early, it meant that we could carry out the vote early, too. So we orchestrated that closure and guess what? The votes are in.'

'Guess what?' Jake grunted from the floor of the cave. 'We don't care.'

'Don't be an idiot, Wilks,' said Harvey. 'This message is a courtesy. It has been decreed that Earth will be destroyed at 6pm this evening, by ultrasonic missiles. You may wish to use your time more *wiresly* than spend your last few hours in an underground cave engaged in the most fruitless of escapades.'

'You mean *wisely*?' Jake said. 'You may wish to use your time more wisely.'

'Sure, whatever,' Harvey said.

'Why should you say that our efforts down here be *fruitless*?' asked Mr Harrison.

Harvey held out a hand, upon which a black metal ornament appeared. It was shaped like a horse's head and contained a bracket at the neck end.

'What is it?' asked Dana.

'Why don't you ask your glorious leader?' suggested Harvey.

Mr Carter cleared his throat. 'Aha… It's an Indicator. There are twenty of them that fix to the circular base of the Paddle. They conduct a current from one to the next and produce the shield that intercepts the blast. You need all of them to make the shield. You can't have a gap in the current.'

'Well, he only has one,' said Mr Harrison. 'Don't you have a spare?'

'I'm afraid not,' said Mr Carter. 'It's all second-hand kit, you see.'

Mr Harrison looked as though his eyes were going to pop out of their sockets. He contented himself by saying, 'You really are something else.'

A disembodied voice called to Harvey from the invisible background of his location. He looked around then turned back to the crestfallen bunch in the cave. 'Best of luck to you all, and remember, use your time *wiresly*.' A tall figure with piercing blue eyes, that Ellie instantly recognised from the *Pablucto Choloros* message, appeared at Harvey's shoulder. Ellie felt her chest tighten as she and Samuel Le Dich met eyes for the briefest of moments, before the hologram disappeared altogether.

'You arrogant fool!' Mr Harrison was yelling at Mr Carter.

'Steady on,' said Mr Carter. 'I was the only one who even considered that the spy could be one of the students. Everyone else was looking at me!'

'Yes,' said Mr Harrison, 'you came to that superb realisation all on your own but didn't stop to think that the spy might be under your very nose, attending your class and stealing your materials!'

Mr Adlington spoke up in an attempt to diffuse the situation, and as the three men talked over each other,

Dana and Ellie exchanged looks of disbelief. Jake was still moaning on the ground, and eventually the collective noise grew to such a crescendo that nobody heard the lift open for the second time.

'*What is going on here?!*'

Everybody froze, their mouths agape.

'The students are on the busses,' said Mrs Atkinson. 'The school is empty. Shall we get a move on?'

Mrs Atkinson sat in Mr Carter's office an hour later, nursing her head in her hands. He was going over with her again every inch of the visit they had had from Harvey, as well as the prize piece of information that Harvey had stolen one of the indicators, throwing their rescue plan into question. 'Now,' he said, 'it's only a piece of metal. Theoretically, we could make a replacement. It's just a question of fixing it to the hull. The Indicators are designed with special brackets that fit perfectly. It'll be tricky to recreate that.'

Mrs Atkinson looked at him. 'I don't really want to hear this,' she said.

'Well, I'm sorry, but—'

'No,' she said. 'No "buts" please, and "I'm sorry" is no good to me whatsoever. I want you to just build the thing.' He looked at her, trying to decide what to say next, but before he could decide, she continued, 'Yes, it might not work. But you know what's never going to work? Sitting around, feeling sorry for ourselves. You've got… what time is it?'

'Ten thirty,' said Mr Carter.

'Ten thirty. You've got...' she looked up to the ceiling and counted quickly under her breath, 'seven and a half hours to intercept that blast. Can it be done?'

'No,' said Mr Carter, 'not without Grip Wires.'

Mrs Atkinson groaned. 'What?'

'The Paddle has to travel at the speed of light,' said Mr Carter. 'The only thing that will hold a makeshift Indicator in place instead of a purpose-built bracket is...' He stared off into space, replaying Harvey's message in his head. 'Wires,' he said slowly. 'Of course! He said *wiresly*, not *wisely*. It's a coded message.'

'What are you talking about?' Mrs Atkinson said.

'I need Ellie,' said Mr Carter, leaping to his feet and tearing back down the corridor to the main cave.

Ellie, Jake and the rest of the group had continued with the building as instructed, but perhaps not with quite the same level of enthusiasm as before. The Paddle was looking like a water droplet now and they were fixing the hatch and boarding ladder to the hole at the back. In spite of this, their spirits were gloomy.

'Ellie!' yelled Mr Carter as he sprang into the cave. 'I need you.' Ellie nodded, brimming with curiosity. 'Harvey said we needed to spend our time *wiresly*. He deliberately mispronounced *wisely*.'

Ellie stared at him in amazement. 'So...'

'Well, I need a special kind of wire to make this work. Did Harvey have a special hiding place, or somewhere you can think of that he might stash something like this?' Slowly, Ellie began to shake her head.

Curiosity significantly aroused, the rest of the group

began to gather around. 'If you have these wires, you could fix the Indicators?' Mr Harrison asked.

'That's right,' said Alexi Carter. 'These particular wires constrict to such an extent that they can withstand space travel. Harvey knew this. He knew something, anyway. It's a message within the message.'

'Come on,' Mr Harrison said. 'That's a bit of a stretch, isn't it? Besides, it may be some kind of double bluff. We can't trust him.'

Alexi Carter barked without even looking at him, 'What choice do we have?'

Mr Harrison considered this, then turned to Ellie. 'Think, now,' he said. 'This could save us all!'

'He didn't have a secret place,' signed Ellie.

Mr Carter saw the sorrow in her face and tried not to look too disappointed.

But Jake's expression cleared and he spoke up. '*He* may not have had a secret place, but *we* do, Ellie.' Ellie stared at him. 'Don't you remember?' Jake went on. 'We erm… we *borrowed* that wire we found to secure our treehouse in place.'

'Treehouse?' said Mr Harrison. 'Not in the forest? That's a restricted area!'

'Shut it,' said Mr Carter and Mr Adlington simultaneously.

Ellie nodded as she remembered the incident Jake was talking about. They had taken the wire that had been left over from a repair job on the perimeter fence. She looked at Mr Carter. 'What kind of wire?' she signed.

'It's called Grip Wire,' he said.

Ellie and Jake looked at each other excitedly and made a dash to the lift. 'Follow us,' called Jake. The whole group started forward, but Mr Carter turned on the other three and said firmly, 'I need you all to stay here and fix that hatch door. Finish the build. Dana, you look after them.' Dana smiled and saluted him like a soldier.

As the lift doors slid open at ground level, they sprinted across the deserted main hall of Oakham Elementary.

Ellie was through the door of the main entrance first, Jake and Mr Carter following close behind. She was headed straight for the perimeter fence. Alexi Carter surveyed the fence that rose high up over their heads and slackened his pace in mingled curiosity and concern. 'How're we gonna get through there?' he wondered aloud. But as he drew nearer Ellie ducked down to a hole at the bottom of the fence that looked for all the world as though it had to have been purpose-built. She crawled through to the grass beyond and beckoned for them both to follow her. 'Of course,' said Mr Carter, fixing Jake with a sardonic eye, 'how silly of me.'

It felt to Jake and Ellie that a lifetime had passed since they had last been into the forest during daylight hours. The space was almost unrecognisable to them, to the point that they nearly passed their tree altogether as they searched the area in haste. 'Here it is,' said Jake in triumph, finally recognising the wider clearing at the base. They each took it in turns to scramble up the trunk of the tree, and when they got to the top, Mr Carter looked around at the wire that bound the wooden planks. It was wrapped round and round the logs and slats in one great length, because Ellie and Jake hadn't ever had the tools to cut it. It was a work of art, woven extremely carefully in and around the woodwork like some great Chinese puzzle. Mr Carter traced every inch of the construction, looking for an end to the wire.

'Didn't you bring wire cutters?' Jake asked.

'No,' said Mr Carter. 'We can't use them. The more you cut Grip Wire, the weaker it becomes. We'll have to unravel it.'

Ellie looked at Jake with a fatalistic air and made the sign for 'typical'.

FIFTEEN

ELLIE LOOKED DOWN at the dismantled remains of her treehouse with sorrow as they lay about her in a mangled heap. It had taken her and Jake the best part of two months to construct the house and just a little over twenty minutes to destroy it. Jake seemed unperturbed as he chatted away with Alexi Carter, coiling Grip Wire in a loop around his hand and his elbow. For Ellie, however, the shattered ruin represented the end of an era. She knew that once they left, she could never come back here.

They walked back to the school together, Jake and Mr Carter discussing the particulars of navigating the Paddle back to Altarc, Ellie mentally saying 'goodbye' to the place she had called home for the last twelve years. She thought of her parents, whose fate was presumed but still unknown. *Goodbye, Mum; goodbye, Dad.*

As they stepped into the lift she watched the doors close in front of her, shutting off her view of the main hall and replacing it with her own slightly distorted reflection. Jake was still quizzing Mr Carter on logistics.

Ellie could see the earnest expression on his face, but she opted out of following the conversation, deciding that she would rather not know the finer details of what was going to happen next.

When the lift touched back down at the basement floor, Ellie felt reassured to see Mr Adlington and Dana putting the final patch of metal work in place. It was her hatch door and she watched proudly as it was guided through the air on a rope and pulley system and slotted neatly into position.

'How about that?' Mr Carter called out encouragingly.

Dana looked over her shoulder and grinned as the three of them entered.

'It just needs welding in place now,' said Mr Adlington. 'I think we will need your blowtorch.'

Mr Carter looked at Ellie and said, 'You can do that if you want. I need to fix this Indicator.' Ellie hastily nodded before he would have a chance to change his mind. 'We'll get you set up with a ladder, then we'll have to lift the whole lot up on those ropes so we can get the Indicators in place.' He turned to Jake. 'Are you alright to give me a hand with that?'

It was with a sigh of bliss that Ellie lowered the mask over her face and fired up the blowtorch. The smell of oil and smouldered metal filled her nostrils as she brought the flame down upon the connecting panels with glee. So engaged was she at her task that when she stepped into the Paddle for the first time an hour later, she half expected to see the interior of a spacecraft with rows and rows of flashing lights on top of a majestic control panel.

It wasn't logical because she knew what the inside would look like if she had really stopped to think about it. When she lowered herself down from the hatch and into one of the seats, a fragment of apprehension began to stir within her. She looked around at the crude finish of the welded sides and the lack of any control panel whatsoever.

It was Jake who voiced the general sentiment as he dropped down into a seat next to her. 'How are we gonna fly this thing?'

'Where're the controls?' Dana asked, following him in and looking up at the dome-like roof.

Mr Carter boarded the Paddle last, looking eagerly around the compartment as he did so. 'They're right here,' he said, pulling a small shard of metal from his pocket. The shard was shaped a little bit like a gherkin and had one button built in at the top.

'How—' Jake began.

'Well, give me a minute and I'll tell you,' said Mr Carter. 'Firstly, there should be an electrical socket somewhere in the floor. Can anyone see that?' They all began to inspect the floor. 'It should just look like a small hole in the ground,' he explained.

'Is this it?' Dana asked, inspecting something near her feet.

'Ah,' said Mr Carter, 'that's it. Well done.' He thrust the gherkin into the hole and pressed the button, which immediately shone with green light. 'Who wants to do the honours?'

They all looked at each other blankly. 'Come on then,' he said to Ellie.

Ellie put her hand out to the button as though she half expected it to shock her, then she looked up at Alexi Carter. 'Now?'

'Don't worry,' said Mr Carter, 'we haven't set a course yet, so it should just hover. Then we can remove the ropes, see.'

Tentatively, Ellie pressed the button. She felt a rumble beneath her feet as the Indicators engaged and jettisoned air to the floor, pushing the Paddle upward a fraction and slackening the rope harness.

'What now?' Jake asked.

'We'll give that a little while to warm up,' said Mr Carter. 'Let's go and get those ropes down.'

They crawled back out of the hatch and down the boarding ladder to the stepladder below. Mrs Atkinson had brought some lunch materials into the cave and she set these down on the floor, placing pillows around for them all to sit on. Ellie hadn't realised how hungry she was, but as they all sat together, cross-legged in a little circle, she picked happily at plates of sausage rolls and sandwiches. Mr Adlington had made a flask of tea, which he divvied up into plastic cups. Ellie drained her tea in seconds flat and held her cup back up to Mr Adlington before he had finished pouring everyone else's out. He laughed, gave her a top-up, then turned to Alexi Carter. 'Have you got plenty of supplies on board?'

'Not a lot,' he admitted. 'I hadn't been anticipating making the trip so soon.' He wiped his beard with a sleeve, dislodging some rogue pieces of pastry and breadcrumb. 'With a bit of luck, we'll be on Altarc in time for tea.'

Ellie, Dana and Jake exchanged excited looks. 'Once we get back, I can have one of the Revelry fleet pick you up, if you want.'

'Just intercept that blast,' said Mr Harrison.

'Agreed,' said Mrs Atkinson. 'First things first.'

It was a strange sensation for Ellie, saying goodbye to her teachers under such extraordinary circumstances. It felt protracted and slightly unnatural. She couldn't really believe what was happening to her. Even when Mr Carter was ushering them into their seats and closing the hatch door, she still didn't believe it. 'Strap yourselves in,' he said. 'We have several floors to pass through.' Ellie sat down in a front seat and pulled a harness from the back, securing it in front of her chest. The interior of the Paddle felt warmer now and the green light on the power socket was now glowing a vibrant orange.

Mr Carter sat down next to her and the atmosphere in the cabin began to hum when he pressed the button of the shard a second time. Jake and Dana took the seats in the row behind and peered over as Mr Carter took a work pad from his jacket pocket and began to enter a code that nobody could begin to interpret. 'Coordinates,' he explained shortly. When he had finished, the screen turned into a live video stream from the Paddle's base. They all craned their necks to look at it. It was their only view of what was happening outside and they could see steam escaping from the sides of the craft.

'I've just realised we don't have any windows,' said Dana. 'Why is that?'

'We're about to get in the way of an ultrasonic missile,' said Alexi Carter. 'It's best that we can't see it coming, believe me.'

'How do we know where it is, then?' Jake said with a frown.

'We don't,' said Alexi Carter. 'That's the beauty of it. The Paddle finds the missile and is drawn to it like a magnet. It is all programmed up. We don't have to guide the Paddle at all.'

Jake opened his mouth to say something else, but Alexi Carter placed a finger over his own and said, 'Shh.' The seats had begun to vibrate. Slowly at first, then harder and harder until they were all rattling so hard neither Jake, Dana nor Ellie could make out the main features of each other's faces anymore. Mr Carter tapped Ellie on the shoulder. She could understand that he was speaking, but for the life of her, she could not fathom what it was that he was saying. All of a sudden there was a jerk. She glanced at the work pad he was still holding in front of him and saw, with a leap of her heart, that they were rising up. Mr Carter adjusted the position of the gherkin-shaped shard and the craft began to rotate on its axis. He said something else that Ellie could not make out, and with another movement of the shard, the Paddle hurtled swiftly upwards towards the roof of the cave. Ellie closed her eyes and braced for impact, but the Paddle burst effortlessly through the workshop ceiling.

Tears gathered at the corners of her eyes and streaked down over her cheeks as they plunged through the ground floor of the school. It was really happening. Ellie thought,

Finally. She gave an involuntary shriek as they passed through the roof of the school. Mr Carter looked at her and smiled, hearing her real voice for the very first time.

The Paddle spun like a top as it rose up into the atmosphere. Within the cabin, Ellie felt as though she were going to throw up. Mr Carter twisted the shard by another forty-five degrees and the Paddle spun faster and faster still. It sped up and up until it was spinning around so fast that it was no longer noticeable. Gravity began to reclaim its purchase on the limbs of the four crew members and slowly, they turned to focus on each other once again.

Grinning, Ellie looked from her friends to the work pad. The video stream showed stars falling away beneath her feet and her toes tingled at the very idea of it. From a corner of the screen, she could see Jake's star. She made an excited grab for his arm and pointed it out to him. 'It looks even better from up here,' he said. Then he had a thought and pointed out the star to Alexi Carter. 'Is that Altarc?'

Mr Carter glanced at the screen and scoffed. 'No,' he said, 'we're better hidden than that. That garish piece of real estate is the safe station.'

Ellie, Dana and Jake stared at it in wonder. 'It's so big,' Dana observed.

'Oh, yeah,' said Mr Carter casually. 'It's proper planet size, alright.' They looked at it for another moment and Ellie considered quite suddenly that it looked revolting. A look of disgust swept across her face as she signed, 'I don't want to go there.'

'That's where your mate is,' teased Mr Carter. Ellie shot him a glance that could have melted iron. 'Sorry.'

He chuckled. 'Seriously, though, he really helped us out.' Ellie waved away Alexi Carter's assessment as though it did not interest her in the slightest. 'He would have taken a big risk to give us a coded message under his father's watch,' persisted Mr Carter.

'So?' Ellie shrugged.

'Just saying,' said Mr Carter. 'You mustn't feel you've been tricked or anything of that nature. Obviously, the affection he felt for you was genuine. He is unfortunately deeply integrated in something much bigger than he can risk violating at this time.'

Ellie again shrugged this off but secretly felt her insides warm a fraction with pride. 'Shouldn't we be doing something?'

Jake voiced her query and Mr Carter looked around at the sparse interior. 'Not really,' he said.

'Is there anything we can do to increase our chances of success?' Jake suggested.

'You can pray if you want,' said Mr Carter, inspecting the work pad in causal aloofness.

'What time is it?' Dana said.

'It's just gone six o clock,' said Mr Carter.

'We'd better get ready!' Jake exclaimed. 'It's gonna happen any minute now.'

'No,' said Alexi Carter. 'The Legion is a stickler for detail. They wouldn't be a minute late.'

'What are you saying?'

'It's already happened,' said Alexi Carter as naturally as if he were talking about the boiling of a kettle.

'What?' Jake shouted. 'So the Earth is destroyed?'

'Well, I'm just trying to gather a progress report now,' said Mr Carter. 'Give me a minute, my machine is a little slow.'

'We don't need a progress report!' Jake screamed. 'Surely we would have felt it if we'd intercepted an ultrasonic missile?'

'Not at all,' said Alexi Carter, scanning the pages of the report. 'The Paddle is built to withstand these blasts. The shield that the Indicators project would prevent us from feeling anything at all. That's what makes Paddles so good.'

They all gaped at him, their mouths hanging open. 'Aha,' he said finally, bringing the work pad closer to his face and reading carefully. 'Oh my goodness!'

Ellie looked at him sharply and signed, 'What is it?'

'Is Earth alright?' Dana called from the back seat.

'Oh, yes,' said Alexi Carter distractedly. 'Earth is fine. We intercepted the blast.' They breathed a collective sigh of relief.

'So what's up?' Ellie signed at him.

Alexi Carter looked at her, knowing what she was asking. 'We appear to have caught the blast pretty much head on,' he said.

'What does that mean?' Jake asked.

'It means that, quite by chance, we sent the missile back to the safe station, by rebound.'

Ellie's heart did a quick somersault. 'Is the safe station alright?'

'It is damaged,' said Alexi Carter.

'Good,' said Jake.

'Not exactly the word I would have chosen,' said Mr Carter.

'Why not?'

'What does this all mean?' asked Dana.

'It means,' said Mr Carter, 'that we've probably angered them slightly and that they may very well be on to us.'

'Shouldn't the Revelry fleet be here soon to rescue us?' Jake said.

'It won't be so easy,' said Mr Carter. 'They would be liable to track us and then our resistance programme would be compromised. There would be a huge amount at stake if they were to do that.'

'So they're just gonna leave us here?' Dana screamed.

'Wouldn't you?' Mr Carter said.

Ellie pointed at the work pad. 'What is that?' A craft of some description was certainly approaching the Paddle. They crammed around the screen.

'It's one of ours,' said Alexi Carter with a modicum of relief. 'It's Revelry One.'

A communications request appeared on the screen, and Alexi Carter swiped to open the channel. 'How're you doing in there, Carter?' a muffled voice asked.

Mr Carter's eyes were alight with joy. 'Very well, thank you, Lottie.' He turned to face Ellie, Dana and Jake, and beamed with pride. 'It's Lottie Richards,' he explained, 'one of the co-founders of the resistance programme, and something of a maverick.'

'Who… gt… n… there with you?' Lottie's broken transmission came through the speaker.

'Three great kids from Oakham Elementary,' said Mr Carter. 'They're looking forward to getting to Altarc as much as I am.'

'Well, come on then,' said Lottie in a clearer transmission. 'I'll come alongside. We're gonna have to take a detour because of the unwanted attention you have drawn to yourselves, but we'll be there soon enough. Prepare for boarding in ten minutes.'

Ellie looked excitedly from Jake to the illustrated soundwaves that danced over the screen to the rhythm of Lottie's words. He carefully relayed to her what he had heard.

'So we're getting out of here?' she signed.

Jake nodded.

Ellie looked back at the screen. Revelry One was making its approach. She could almost see Lottie through the pilot's window, now. She closed her eyes and fell back in her seat, relief coursing through her veins.

Come on, she thought to herself. *Take me to my new home, wherever it may be.*